FSC
www.fsc.org
MIX
Papier aus ver-
antwortungsvollen
Quellen
Paper from
responsible sources
FSC® C105338

Translation by Patricia Magdalena Redlin
Proofread by Nicholas Modlin
Book Cover Design by RockingBookCovers.com

Printed and published by BoD – Books on Demand, Norderstedt
ISBN: 9783750440647

"Stolen Lives"

Part III

Hiam Mondini

The question about the Blackberry is
unnecessary.

For Nicholas

Introduction

A frosty cold north wind sneaks furtively through the narrow streets of the Scottish village and drives people back into their warm houses. Those who can afford it stay inside where it's warm all day long, enjoying the crackling fire in the fireplace, reading exciting stories about distant lands, cooking delicacies and dreaming of the wide world. White sand beaches, warm sand between their toes and well-mixed cocktails at the pool bars. Vacations that only a few can afford, but everyone knows about from movies and travel advertisements. Seductive pictures, day in, day out.

The wooden door of the rustic warehouse opens and a tall, stocky man, weather-beaten and dressed in practical clothes, struggles against the wind and closes the door behind him. With a grim look on his face, he puts both his hands in his jacket pockets and walks with heavy steps toward the free-standing stone house, takes two large pieces of wood from the pile next to the grand staircase and opens the door to the warmth. Without removing his shoes, he shuffles through the spacious entrance to the cozy living room. The cheerfully dancing fire casts a warm light and makes the room look even more stylish. As the tall Scot kneels in front of the fireplace, he hears little feet walking down the stairs. He rolls his eyes and goes over to stand before her, saying, "No boots in the house! How many times do I have to say it! I clean and clean in here and you can't come up with a better idea than to bringing all the dirt from the stinking stable in here! It'll take me another whole day to get that stink out of the house! What will our guests think!" He shoots back a teasing response as he pokes around in the fire.

When he hears neither a contradiction nor an outburst of insults, he turns around, wondering, and looks into the gaping eyes of the petite woman standing in the open door. Slowly he gets up, walks over to her and bends down to her eye level. "You look like you've seen a ghost! Did you see a ghost? Hailey?" The girl blinks excitedly and swallows almost audibly before she finds her voice. "He's coming... They're coming... All... Both... All three of them... They're all coming..."

Chapter 1

"Bonnie, as always, it was just delicious! You're by far the best cook on this planet!" Frank leans back comfortably in his chair, takes the napkin from his lap and slaps his well-muscled stomach with the palm of his hand. "So, it's a good thing I got in two rounds this morning. Otherwise, I won't be getting any more parts in exciting movies, I definitely belong to the old guard in Hollywood, but every meal of yours is worth the difficult physical training, my pearl!" He reaches for Bonnie's hand as she goes to take his plate off the table and gives the old lady an appreciative kiss on it. She pulls her hand away, embarrassed, and replies, "Now stop it! You exaggerate as always! But I'm not saying you're not flattering me. Thank you, Frank!" She picks up his plate and walks around the large mahogany table to take Ken's plate as well.

"No Bonnie, he's not exaggerating! That was really a fantastic meal! I would say a gourmet reviewer would call this a 'palate explosion' and rate it with 5 stars!" He copies the actions of his father and sits back in his chair, also slapping his stomach and smiling as he says, "However, my fitness rounds this morning were not quite as athletic as yours, Dad. I whipped our apartment into shape, ran to the supermarket, took the stairs instead of the elevator, and that's it! Now everything is ready for the big reception."

Frank gets up from his chair and heads for his bar. "Do you also want a little digestif? Otherwise I will explode in mid air!" He laughs happily and takes a bottle of single malt from the mobile globe-shaped liquor cabinet. Ken puts his napkin on the table and stands up from his cozy position. "Dad, I wanted to tell you something before we drive to the airport." He slowly approaches his father, who is holding out a crystal glass with golden liquid contents.

"Drive?"

Chapter 2

She should not have told him. Not yet, at least. But how in the world could she keep such news to herself? Hailey vigorously mashes the still steaming potatoes in the pan. The earthy smell spreads around the large kitchen and gives the experienced cook renewed motivation. Yes, she had to tell him without delay. It would have been a lot worse for him if he would have found out about it in the village. Such news spreads fast and then it's either not true at all or only half of it is. Don't even think about if Crissa had found out before him. "Holy Mother of God!" Hailey crosses herself with a startled look out of the window. She lingers on that thought for a fraction of a second, then eagerly resumes mashing the potatoes. Crissa must not find out – that would be a disaster! Once she gets wind of this gossip, lies will spread all over the village. That would be worse than the plague! Once again, the small Scotswoman crosses herself and begins whispering the Lord's Prayer.

"Whom did you kill?" As if caught in the act, Hailey drops her cooking spoon into the pan, slaps her chest with her hand and turns on her heels. "Do not say such horrible things, Angus Cunningham MacKay! And what in the world do you think you're doing, coming into my clean kitchen with your dirty boots?" She turns around angrily, picking up a knife and lifting it menacingly into the air without even glancing at the man who gave her such a fright. "Go outside and bring me a chicken!" When she doesn't hear any sounds behind her, she slowly turns around and looks directly into the man's grim stare. With his arms crossed in front of his chest, the laird of the manor leans against the door frame and chews on a blade of grass sticking out of his mouth. "I'm not INSIDE the kitchen... I'm standing in the doorway..." He raises an eyebrow casually, snorts air loudly into his nose and stomps one of his boots on the floor.

"You are a monster, Angus Cunningham MacKay! A terrible, misbehaved and godless monster!" Hailey puts down the knife, brushes her hands on her lacy apron, and walks over to the big wooden table in the middle of the kitchen. She takes the scissors lying on top of it, cuts some herbs from the fresh shrubs in their pots and places them gently in a small bowl. After placing it next to the hot pan, she goes to the refrigerator, opens the chromed door, takes out a glass bottle and returns with the bottle full of white liquid to the steaming pan. After unscrewing the milk, Hailey pauses for an instant. She can feel her chest rise and fall for a moment. A second later, she finishes by adding some milk into the mashed potatoes and says loudly, "Well then, I guess there will be no fried chicken today!"

Chapter 3

"But she will hopefully get used to this situation, won't she?" Frank looks out of the limousine window with a slightly bored look on his face and taps a rhythm on his leg with his fingers. Ken grins mischievously and turns to his father, saying, "Are you getting comfortable in your old age? Hey, Dad, a grandfather should be flexible and spontaneous! I thought Mirjam was keeping you in good shape!" The cheerful Law Professor sits down on the side seats in the long limousine so that he can get a better look at his father. He opens his shirt collar slightly and looks at the watch on his wrist. "Hm… Mirjam... When exactly are they landing anyway? I could surprise the little one and we could all meet at home. They're still planning on coming to the guest house, right?" He looks questioningly into the excited eyes opposite him.

"You know what? That's a great idea! Why don't you surprise Mirjam, kidnap her and fly back with her? We can take the car and drive to Roberto's office and take him with us. Then we all meet at home. And yes, we would like to use the guest house for a few days. Then we'll go back to the city. Ok, Dad?"

His father's raised eyebrows and twisted mouth tell Ken that only part of his idea has been well received by the nation's former action hero. And he tries another tactic to get his father's facial expression to change. "Come on, Dad, we'll enjoy a vacation together soon! And believe me, you will be glad to get some rest away from us later!"

Frank Conley clicks his tongue and casually presses the button next to him. Kenneth rolls his eyes, leans his head back and pushes his butt forward to the edge of the seat so that he's hanging off the seat like a potato sack. "Here we go..."

The darkened window between the driver's compartment and the back of the stretch limo is slowly opening and now the view of the road in front of them and the neck and right shoulder of Max the driver are visible. "Hey my friend! Tell me, how are your boys? All healthy and cheerful? Is your Melissa still the happiest woman in the world?" Frank speaks these words into the built-in microphone next to his seat. His longtime driver and companion on the streets of New York looks into the rearview mirror, with a pleased look, and answers, "Of course, sir! All happy and healthy! Melissa is getting prettier by the day and my boys make us proud parents of college students, sir! You know, this is all because we don't live in this stinking city. Children need fresh air and sea breeze to thrive and be healthy! Like you, Mr. Conley Junior!" He winks in the rearview mirror and slides the window separator silently up again.

Chapter 4

"Good boy! Let's find some peace and quiet. I have never enjoyed female chatter." Angus pulls the

15

girth on his stallion a little tighter and gently strokes the horse's shiny black fur. He takes the reins in his hand and swings skillfully and casually onto the back of the strong animal. The clicking of his tongue and a light kick with his foot let the trained horse know which way to go. The two ride comfortably away from the farm, through the forest path alongside the babbling brook, out over the vast, hilly landscape of the Scottish Highlands. They don't start to trot until the stallion feels the need to put more power into his legs, and then they gallop up to the high cliffs. An indescribable view down to the ocean presents itself and Angus brings his obedient horse to a halt.

"What would I do without you, my dear boy?" Angus taps his big hand on the strong neck of his faithful companion and lets his gaze wander over the sea. "What do you think about us having some visitors?" The animal who's being asked shakes his shiny mane and snorts loudly. "Hm, yes... I feel the same way! I don't particularly like having the house full of people. Especially not, when the same old stories get told again and again. Hailey will be reminded of everything again and she's already finding it difficult to sleep. Well, she will have to stop doing that now because she knows they're coming. She would never admit it, you know, but I'm not as introverted as she constantly insists I am. You know that, right? And shall I tell you why I know she can't sleep well? Her scrambled eggs are overcooked, not spicy enough or too spicy, her tea is brewed too long, the coffee is much too strong, the meat is fried until it's the consistency of shoe leather and the salad is swimming in dressing!"

He picks up the reins and gives his silent listener a few gentle kicks in the side. They gallop along the stunningly beautiful landscape and back home. A breathtaking home, that has been maintained and nurtured for generations, as far as Angus can see in his Scottish family tree that hangs on the wall of the large staircase. And no one will ever change that…if only the issue with his offspring were not so difficult.

Chapter 5

After the long vehicle parked in front of the airport has unloaded a passenger, it is driven back to Brooklyn. Frank Conley presses a key on his BlackBerry and holds it to his ear. "Hey Tom, how are you? Do you have time for a former customer?" He laughs and stretches his long legs out. "Great! No, thanks, I do not want to smell studio air. I'd rather inhale your fresh leather seats! Ha-ha…exactly! I need a driver for the little wild one and me. I'm on my way to school with Max right now. But he has to pick Ken up from the airport. Yes, exactly… They are arriving today. It's unbelievable, right?" He looks out the window and realizes that they will soon be arriving at their destination. "Alright then, in front of the school? And then we'll get going to meet Mike at the airfield! You are still the best! See you soon!"

The tall, still very well-built actor thanks his driver and gets out of the limousine. He closes the top two buttons of his jacket and walks elegantly, one hand casually in his trouser pocket, toward the school entrance. He opens the big entry door, then the next door to the reception office at the private school.

"Hello, ladies," he calls to the women who are already looking up from behind the counter, and they both stand up as if the commander of a police academy had entered.

"Hello Mr. Conley! How nice to see you! Somebody will be happy about this surprise!" The older of the two finds her voice first and pushes a sheet of paper over to him. "May I ask you to sign here? I'll do everything else, a blind autograph, so to speak." As she says that with a delightful smile, the younger girl giggles into her hand and leans back in her chair in embarrassment. Frank signs on the line for his signature and secretly enjoys the effect he still has, even though his movie days are now a long time in the past.

"Donna, will you take Mr. Conley to the classroom, please?" The first secretary takes the sheet off the counter and points out the direction to the young silly girl the way with her pen.

"Of course, I'd love to! Would you like to follow me, Mr. Conley?" She gets up, walks around the counter, and opens the second door of the office behind glass panes.

"Please, call me Frank. Mr. Conley sounds so old." The big, self-confident man, holds the door open now so the small secretary can scurry through, taking a deep breath of his seductive aftershave. She giggles again and replies, "I'd love to, sir! Oh... I mean Frank, of course."

Chapter 6

"Here you are at last! Do you still need more time with the horses?" Hailey stands with both hands on her hips in the open stall door. Angus calmly rests on one bent knee, trimming one of the horses' hoof. "Yes, here I am, Hailey. What do you need?" Slowly he puts the horse's leg back down on the ground, letting his hand slide over the leg and gently slapping the animal's hind end. "Good girl!" He takes the rag from the half-open wooden door next to him and wipes his hands with it.

"I would like to go to the village. Can you accompany me? Please?" Her hands folded as if in prayer, she now appears almost shy.

"And what do you need from the village? Can't Sam get it?" He takes the saddle next to him off the beam and goes back to the stately white mare. He then hangs the elegant saddle on a designated hook in front of the mare. The beautiful horse starts to get restless, so he strokes her neck under the wild mane and soothes her, "It will be fine..."

"No, Angus, you don't understand. I would like to go to the village with YOU. I need decent clothes and would like to have lunch at Bynnie's." No sooner has she finished talking, she hears deep, murmuring sounds from the horse stall with the new young mare. "Please Angus... I can't receive them this way, wearing these old rags. What will they think!" She blows her nose with the kitchen towel hanging out of her apron and walks slowly away from the stable.

"What do you want me to wear to go to Bynnie's?" Angus is leaning against the stable door, brushing his hands, with his eyes fixed on them. Hailey stops walking but does not turn to face him, so that he will not notice her happy smile, and replies, "The blue turtleneck I knit you for Christmas and the beige corduroy trousers. No boots! Your church shoes." Her face still radiant, she triumphantly approaches the house and hears the deep male voice behind her.

"Clean underdrawers as well?"

Chapter 7

Frank stops in front of the classroom door and thanks his companion. "Thank you, Donna. I'll wait a bit longer and watch the kids through the window. I like watching young and eager students. Is that ok?" He looks at her questioningly. "I'm sorry, Mr. Conley, Frank, I'm not allowed to leave you alone in the hallway, but I would love to wait with you, if you want. I have time." She blinks, slightly embarrassed, then looks through the window in the door into the classroom. "Oh look, it's Mirjam's turn! They are having their blood types checked today. Isn't that exciting? Back in my day, we didn't do such cool things in physics and biology classes. Mostly, we just studied leaves on trees, dissected rabbits and memorized some stupid tables."

"What do you mean; they're checking their blood types?" Conley frowns and looks into the room, where a group of students is gathered around a large table. "What are they doing? Is that blood? HER blood?!" Now looking shocked, he moves his face closer to the window and before Donna can answer, Frank opens the door with a jerk. "Hey! What exciting things are you doing there?!" He shouts, and all heads turn around to him.

"Skipper! What are YOU doing here?!" The smallest girl with dark long curls joyfully drops her sterile instruments and hops over to the visitor. She hugs him and is immediately hugged back. Frank kisses her on the head and breathes in the scent of her hair. "Mmm, how I missed you, Lassie!" He pinches her waist, which makes her giggle.

"Mr. Conley, what an honor to welcome you to our experimentation lesson!" The tall, thin teacher, who is wearing an orange T-shirt and washed-out jeans, steps over to the two, who are still hugging each other. He shakes Frank's hand in greeting. "You have a strong handshake, sir. Who would have thought it?" Frank winks at him and replies, "I hope I am not bothering you!" As he says this, he looks curiously at the table and the items lying on it.

"No, not at all, sir! Please, come closer! Mirjam was preparing her blood for a check. Now we will have to wait until next time. But that's not a problem, is it?" The science teacher looks first at Conley, then at Mirjam, who shakes her head eagerly, saying, "No, no, it's fine!" She goes over to the table and takes the flat plate with the red spot on it in her hand. "I still have enough of it." She laughs happily and throws the plate into the lockable bucket under the table.

The astonished visitor goes over to the table and asks, "Why are you throwing it away?"

"Because the blood has dried up now!" A blond girl standing next to Frank answers his question. "It's my turn now!" She eagerly reaches for the microscope and carefully opens a small tube with some red liquid in it.

Chapter 8

Silently they sit side by side in the old Cadillac and drive through the untouched landscape of the Highlands. Happy and a bit nervous, Hailey sits bolt upright. Her outfit is white leather and her delicate hands, enclosed in cream-colored gloves, lie on her handbag, which is the same color. After driving over a stone that causes the car to shake briefly, she straightens her hat that covers part of her white curls. With a reproachful look on her face, she turns to Angus and stares at him sideways. He casually raises his shoulders and murmurs, "I didn't put him out on the street." He leans his head on his right fist, with his arm leaning against the window.

"Shouldn't you keep both hands on the steering wheel?" His nervous passenger turns to look at him pointedly.

"Someone who can't even drive has nothing to complain about!" He does not pay any attention to her, just continues to look at the road in front of him.

"How can you be such an old grump! You never talked like this to..." She just barely shakes her head and looks out the window at the landscape again. "You know, Angus, it's not easy for me either. I would have liked things to be a bit differently as well. But you're a grown man now and a very good participant. You can't always stay out here alone. And I won't be around for all of eternity and...and..." She can't finish her tirade, because the driver interrupts her, "And I also have to put up with a diaper shitter!"

"Angus Cunningham MacKay! Do not talk about your descendant like that! What exactly are you thinking should happen here anyhow? What have I done wrong in your upbringing?" Outraged, the small Scotswoman turns on the seat, so that her back is facing Angus.

After a long pouting silence, she sits straight again, smooths her coat and clears her throat, saying, "Well, I didn't do everything wrong! You will see, you'll like her." As soon as she finishes the sentence, the silent listener steers the car to the side of the road and turns off the engine.

"Angus?! What are you doing?! Is something wrong with the car? Why are we stopping here?" Puzzled, she looks first out the window and then back at her companion, who is sitting quietly behind the wheel, his eyes still on the road in front of them, slowly sliding his tongue over his upper lip before he purses his lips as if he wants to whistle. He inhales loudly and clicks his tongue. "Angus, what's going on here?" Hailey leans over towards him.

"You tell me! What is the real reason, I changed into fresh underwear?"

Chapter 9

"That was a great class! The teacher seems to be very nice! Do you like him, Lassie?" Frank steps nervously from one foot to the other. "Yes, I like him very much, he's super nice and always doing such cool things with us!" Mirjam stands in front of the big

27

man whom she has called Skipper ever since she first learned how to talk. She winks at him, saying, "What's going on up there? Why are you so nervous?"

Frank stands firmly on both feet, puts his big hands on her petite shoulders and looks into her dark eyes. "Because some important visitors are arriving today! Big and small, wild and quiet, young and old! Do not say you forgot, Lassie! Not you! After all, you are the smartest person in the family! There's quite a brain inside that beautiful head, right?" Smiling, he taps his forehead with his finger. She grabs his finger lightning-fast and opens her mouth silently. She pauses for a few seconds, then replies, "Today? They're coming today? Are they already here? Where are they?!" She's still holding his finger and starts looking at the street, the parking lot and the school entrance. Right at this moment, a red Porsche drives up and the darkened window on the passenger side is lowered. She does not recognize the person behind the wheel, but hears a familiar voice say, "Who needs to urgently get to the airfield?"

Joyfully, the teenage girl jumps up and runs over to the red luxury car. "Me, me, take me with you, Tom!" She opens the passenger door and sticks her head in. "Hi Tom! Wow, is this new? Is it yours?" She looks around inside the car. "Yes, it's mine. Do you like it? Get in the back seat and we'll also take the lost old man behind you!" He laughs heartily and pats the seat next to him, saying, "Need some help, action hero?!"

At the airfield, the two men give each other a friendly hug before Mike opens the helicopter door for Mirjam. "My lady, welcome on board!"

He then turns to Frank, grinning. "Would you like to climb the stairs, sir?" He ducks just in time to dodge Frank's flying fist. "Oh, that would have caught me sharp! The stunts give way!" He shakes his head theatrically and walks around his flying workplace to get in the pilot's seat.

"So, today is the big day, I heard! Is there a tourist flight in the next few days? Should I come up with something fun?" The Conleys' long-time pilot focuses on the metropolitan landscape in front of them and presses a couple of buttons, Mirjam's voice can be heard in the headset as she says, "Unfortunately no, she's terribly afraid of flying, so that's why it has taken so long for her to finally visit us. I cannot wait to see the twins again. They have definitely grown a ton over these past few weeks."

Chapter 10

Silently, the guests sit at a small round table at the cozy Bynnie's. Hailey first observes the nice woman at the table, then Angus, who looks out of the window, bored. She rolls her eyes, grabs a piece of bread from the basket between them and breaks the silence. "Well then, tell us, Stacy. What brings you here? Up here to see us in the north, I mean. You are from Glasgow, right?" The young woman being addressed puts her hands on the table and looks at Hailey with a friendly smile, replying, "That's right, I'm from the city and I have always wanted to go to the countryside. I did not realize it was so far north, but it's very nice here, I like it very much." Embarrassed, she too reaches for a piece of bread, tears off a small piece and puts it in her mouth. She looks at Angus from the side and slowly chews the bread.

Hailey notices that she would like to ask him something and starts speaking again. "Angus, remember the last time we were in Glasgow? Um, it must surely have been 18 years ago, right?" When he does not react to her question, she turns back to the guest at the table. "It was a great vacation. You know, my sister was here with my grandnephew. And I wanted to go do something with them away from the farm." As she begins to tell the story, Angus clears his throat and interrupts her. "I don't think our vacations are all that exciting to a stranger. When will our food come? Are the animals freshly slaughtered after people order their meals?" He says this last sentence so loud that the guests at the next table turn to look at them.

"Angus?? Angus Cunningham MacKay??! Is that really you?! I'll milk a cow on the spot! What are you doing here? Did one of your horses get lost?!" Laughing, a man stands up and walks towards the big Scot, who does not move but looks out of the window again. The man pats him on the shoulder and sits down on the empty chair at the table without being asked. He glances around and nods his head, saying, "Ladies! Oh, hello, Hailey! I did not recognize you in that elegant dress! I only recognized this old rogue here! Did you drag him out? He certainly doesn't appear to be happy about it!" Amused, he shows his yellow teeth through his dense, orange beard and bangs his fist on the table. "Hey, boy! When are you going to be around again? I heard you bought the wild mare from Stirling! Are you getting her trained and ready?"

Angus looks behind the man who is bombarding him with questions and raises his arms in the air, saying, "Well finally! I was afraid I was going to starve here. Come on, bring it over!" He has barely taken the full plate from the waitress when he hears Hailey say softly, "Angus, please!" He sets the plate filled with hot food on the table in front of him and murmurs, "Well, what the hell. A bit of conversation won't hurt me today." He picks up his knife and fork, waits politely until the two women have their received food, cuts off a piece of his still bleeding steak and looks at his challenger. "You are disturbing me at my meal and while I am on a date with my lady friends! I'll see you at the tournament." He looks at the two women at the table, nods to them and before he puts the piece of meat in his mouth, he says, "Ladies, bon appetit!"

Chapter 11

"Bonnie!!!" Mirjam sees the older woman, who is standing in front of the house, from the landing site. She grabs her backpack, throws it over her shoulder and starts running. "Bye Mike, and thanks for the flight!", she calls back and leaves. Frank walks slowly around the helicopter next to his pilot and puts both hands in his pockets. "These young people nowadays! Full of energy and power! You would not believe what they just pulled off in the classroom, Mike!" The pilot looks over at him, blinking, and asks, "Do I want to know?" Frank laughs out loud, puts his hand on Mike's shoulder and replies, "Maybe not. You still need to stay fully concentrated today!" He pats Mike's shoulder and looks towards the house. "I need to do something else with you and our fear-of-flying guest. Either you're a Conley or you're not!" He slaps the pilot's shoulder a little harder as a goodbye and turns toward the house.

Mirjam's childish chatter can already be heard on the veranda as Frank opens the big French window. "Hey, Lassie, we still need Bonnie! You can't keep chattering to her until you wear her out!" He then addresses Bonnie. "Did Ken get in contact with you?"

Bonnie holds Mirjam's tiny hands tightly, smiling from ear to ear. "Yes, he did. Everything went well. They were just on their way to the family office and then they're coming here." She takes a look at her small wristwatch and adds, "They will definitely be here soon! You were at school for a long time. Did you do something fun?" She asks Mirjam this question and squeezes her hands. "Oh Bonnie, it's so exciting what we're doing in science class! Did you know that you might have lots of nationalities in you? Well, in your blood, actually! Did you know that, Bonnie? Just imagine – it could be that one of your ancestors was Greek or Italian or French! Did you know that?"

Mirjam's renewed chattering and very excited demeanor allow Bonnie and Frank to exchange glances unnoticed. Frank shrugs his shoulders and raises eyebrows, which provide enough clues for his Scottish housekeeper. "Aye, Aye, I've heard that before. I think I saw something on television how many people visited their homeland countries after they learned where their ancestors all came from. And you are doing the same thing in school? No wonder you stayed so long." She looks at Conley understandingly and then turns back to the little experimentalist, "Come on, we'll set up your room here and I'll tell you everything Skipper did as a teenager to avoid sitting at his school desk at any cost. You cannot imagine what he did on our farm back then to distract us from school and make a huge impression on my niece!"

Chapter 12

After Angus has stowed all the bags in the trunk, he lets his eyes wander over the village street and the shops. He cleans his nose noisily with a cloth handkerchief and murmurs into it, "I would have to die here!" He puts the handkerchief back in his trouser pocket and goes over to the driver's door. As she gets in the car, Hailey begins babbling at him. "Isn't she adorable? And she has such good manners! And she's so smart! A veterinarian! Would you ever have imagined it? She was assigned to come here exclusively because her Diters... Disser... Oh never mind, that book, the book she wrote was so good! And she's still so young!" She puts both hands in her lap and continues talking as Angus starts the engine. He interrupts her and says, "Hailey, I was sitting at the table!"

"Exactly! You were also sitting at the table! And what did you do? Shoveled your food into your mouth, staring out the window and not even looking at Stacy at all! On the contrary, you even chased Ian out, but he just wanted to show you his interest!" At these words, Angus laughs out loud, which appears to surprise Hailey. "Showing interest – that's a good one! The old jerk wants my mare. He just didn't have enough money to buy her, and now he's afraid he won't get a title again. What he should do for once is take care of the animals he has. He has no idea, no idea! It's a shame for any good farm, what he shows..." He shakes his head and puts his hand casually on the steering wheel.

"And you will also soon run out of money if you don't plan for the future! You can't do this alone for much longer! What, or who would be more appropriate than a veterinarian?! Don't you see it? It's no coincidence Angus that she landed here so far up north!"

She takes off her gloves, puts them carefully on top of her bag and looks up at the street in front of them with her head held high. "Well, that's enough for today. Let's just let it go for now. You obviously didn't scare her too much. I wonder whether she likes light or nutritious cuisine? ... Hmm... I will certainly use the good china. Then she will immediately see that your dishes don't look as nasty as your mouth!"

Her driver takes a deep breath and replies, "She is not coming to eat, she wants to see the horses. Sam will do his best to show her the clean stall, the wonderful leather tack and my great beauties. And he will also be happy about a delicious meal prepared by you. I would guess he likes nutritious cuisine. The china won't be so important then. But even if you enjoy polishing silver for hours, don't go to that much trouble. I don't know yet if I will have time for the society ladies. Someone has to worry about the oh-so-important future. The competition will be here soon."

Chapter 13

The black stretch limousine drives slowly along the magnificent, round driveway. The crunch of the light-colored pebbles sounds majestic and is always a sign that someone is coming home. The big gate closes as if by magic behind the car and the heavy wooden door to the staircase opens.

"They're here! Skipper! Bonnie! They're here!" Excitedly, the teenage girl hops barefoot down the white steps and stops on the bottom step. The driver's door and one of the passenger doors open at the same time. The driver rushes quickly to open the other door as well, waving Mirjam over.

"Welcome home, Mrs. Conley." He starts to offer the woman his hand, but she thanks him, refuses it, and gets out of the car.

A loud shriek is heard as Bonnie and Frank step out of the front door. "Hey, hey!!! You'll wake up all the neighbors! Old people are still sleeping at this time!" Frank stretches his arm theatrically in one direction, then immediately spreads both arms and crouches down. "Come here my savages! Baba needs kisses now, immediately!" Four short, chubby children's legs fight their way up the big steps and joyful children's shouts can now be heard. "Baba! Baba! Baba!" Four fleshy little arms try to grab the big shoulders, neck and head of their emotional grandfather. "Heavens, you have gotten big! What are they feeding you in Mexico!?" He purposely moves backwards and encloses the two children firmly in his strong arms.

Bonnie walks happily past this spectacle and down the stairs. "Bonnie! Oh my Bonnie! How I have missed you!" The petite woman in a white summery lace dress walks over to the tiny Scotswoman, arms outstretched, and hugs her heartily.

"And I have also missed you, Mrs. Conley! I missed you all! I can't even begin to describe what the old man standing back there went through!" The two women pull away from their embrace as Mirjam wriggles her way between them.

"Bonnie, you still have to meet someone, come on!" Her excitement is immediately interrupted. "Mirjam! First help Skipper with the boys!" Laughing, an elegantly dressed woman gets out of the limousine, approaches Bonnie and hugs her as well. "Bonnie, so nice to see you!" Her embrace is returned, and she is looked over from head to toe. "My dear, is there nothing to eat in the city?! Christ, Bob, where are you?! What are you doing with my Linda?!"

Chapter 14

The magnificent car drives elegantly through the romantic forest to the large courtyard entrance. From a distance, the two inmates see the young stable boy sitting on the fence. "What is Sam doing here? Did you forget to tell him we're going to the

40

village? Oh no, poor boy! Who knows how long he has been sitting there waiting for you?" Distraught, as if something terribly bad has happened, Hailey holds both hands over her mouth. Nothing much can be heard anymore from Angus than a low growl. He drives the car slowly over to the hedge and opens his window. "That's not a seat, Sam!" He keeps the engine running and looks towards the house. The stable boy hops down from the fence and bends over next to the open driver's window without touching the car. "Excuse me, sir. I did not want to miss you when you got home."

"Go! Make yourself useful! Get Abbey and Aaron ready. I'll be right back." With these words, Angus closes the window again and steers the car to the manorial house.

Shaking her head, Hailey grabs Angus's hand and lets him help her get out of the car. "You know what, I give up! There is no point in trying to change you! You are who you are, and I will not let myself age even faster because of your behavior! I just wish you would at least go to a little trouble!" She hangs her purse on her arm and smooths out her coat. "I assume you'll bring Sam to dinner with you later? At least, this emaciated boy should get something to eat if he was already here for nothing!" She turns to the stone staircase and ascends the stairs slowly and carefully.

"Certainly, m'lady!" Angus replies behind her back, bowing as he closes the car door.

"I still have eyes in the back of my head! You always forgot that as a child! Only your sister was smart enough to remember!" She unlocks the big wooden door and enters the house.

"Exactly, what a smart girl she was! Especially when she married her own murderer!" Angus murmurs to himself and wanders over to the stable.

Chapter 15

"I still can't believe how tall you are! Time goes by way too fast, right? I was just holding a baby in my arms and in the blink of an eye, decisions about which university to attend are being made!" Linda takes a crystal glass filled with bubbling champagne and reaches for another. She walks over to her husband and holds it out to him. "Would you like one too, Habibi?"

Roberto's right hand grabs it while his left hand holds the brake of his wheelchair. "With pleasure, my beauty! Even though, after such a day at work, I tend to reach for something stronger." He winks at Frank, who is putting the bottle of Moet back on the silver tray.

"Well, I can still remedy that! Then I won't have to drink this princess piss! Excuse me, my dear, I know you like this stuff!" He raises his hands defensively in the air and goes to his fancy bar in the next room. "Tell me, Roberto, how's it going at your doctor's office?" Frank returns with two filled whisky glasses, hands one of them to Roberto and sits down on a comfortable leather chair opposite him. Linda heads for the kitchen and raises her glass. "I will help Bonnie. It seems like the kids in the guest house need a bit more time."

"It's going well, very well, actually, Frank! And I am still deeply in your debt!" The Swiss man in the wheelchair lifts his whisky glass. "Sláinte!"

"Sláinte!" replies the big Scotsman and both men take a sip with relish. "You are not in the least in my debt! And you know that very well. What would I have without you? No wild grandchildren, no charming daughter-in-law and a new monster-in-law!" He laughs out loud and taps his leg with his hand. "No, all joking aside. She seems to be a wonderful woman! What do you think, Rob, can you help her?" He takes another sip from the glass before placing it on the small table next to him.

"You know I'm not a specialist in this field, but I have good contacts here. The fact is, I have already mentioned it to a colleague at last week's conference. But I wanted to wait to drop the bomb until we're eating..." He sips from his glass and squints towards the kitchen. "I have not told Linda about it yet, and you know how she reacts when it comes to secrets!" He rolls his eyes and smiles mischievously.

"Oh... that's nasty! Come on! Out with the announcement! What good are you?!" Conley Senior braces his elbows on his legs and leans forward curiously.

Chapter 16

Angus confidently enters the stable wearing his riding outfit. He goes to the two saddled horses and grabs the reins of his beautiful stallion. Sam walks over and looks at the laird in surprise. "You're riding Aaron, sir?" He clumsily stops beside the white mare and lays his hand gently on her neck.

"Sam, how long have you been working for me?" The stately man now picks up Abbey's reins and leads both horses out of the stable. Embarrassed, the stable boy, who is no longer a boy, walks beside them and answers, "About three years, sir, I think. I haven't counted. Is it important?" Slightly irritated, he plays with the leather strap of the saddle.

"Stop doing that! You're making her more nervous than she already is! So three years, huh...

and you still do not know how to train a new horse?" He stops and looks at his helper sternly. "And now tell me! What did you find out about the tournament?"

***

Angus sits elegantly on his faithful companion, with Abbey beside them, as they ride through his forest, away from the yard. Again and again he makes snapping noises and speaks to his beautiful animals. "Good girl! You'll be home soon. You'll see. Right, Aaron? We also had problems at first and look at us both today!" He pats the black horse happily on the neck, who answers with a nod and a snort. "You see, Abbey, we know what we're talking about and you're a very special and most elegant lady! Yes, that's what you are! You should have seen the greedy eyes of this Ian character today! It's unbelievable how much time humanity wastes on stupid chattering. He almost put me off my food. Hm, it was basically okay, but of course, it cannot compare to the food our Hailey prepares. No one outdoes her cooking, except maybe... No, definitely not! That poor woman has to cook using American crap! They certainly can't get our fresh,

46

good Scottish ingredients over there!" He nods his head and looks up in the direction of heaven and then clicks his tongue again. "I think that's enough for today, my friends! Let's not let Sam wait too long. For you, my beauty, there is still some tightrope dancing waiting." He turns both horses on their own axes and they return purposefully back to the yard.

"Sam! Come here! Show what you've learned!" MacKay tethers his stallion by the fence to the paddock and walks in with the excited mare. The stable boy comes out of the big wooden house, accompanied by a young woman in a black riding outfit.

"Hello, Angus! I hope I am not a bother watching you!"

Chapter 17

"Bonnie, the guesthouse looks gorgeous! How are you able to do it every time, making sure everything is perfect? I can barely make my kitchen look like a kitchen!" The cheerful Mexican woman approaches Bonnie, who is busy fussing around in the large, open-plan kitchen. As the visitor tries to lift a pan lid, Bonnie moves quickly over to her, lays her hand over the woman's, and looks at her affectionately, saying, "I only have ONE child to look after, while you have three and you are doing a great job of it! But in here, my dear, you haven't lost anything. You are welcome to go sit with Linda." She points the kitchen spoon in the other direction of the spacious kitchen, where Linda sits, grinning, on a stool and plays with her champagne glass. "Yes, come over here to me, Rosa. This is the corner for those of us who have been banned!" With a sigh, the dainty woman, who is now among those banned from the kitchen, accepts the invitation and sits next to Linda on another stool.

"And how do YOU manage it, Linda? Look at you! You are always perfect! Everything is always perfect with you! Perfect family, perfect house, perfect doctor's office, perfect child, perfect car..." Her list is interrupted by her husband, who has entered the kitchen in the meantime.

"Hey, hey, hey! Let's talk about something a bit more decent in here now! Starting with you, Bonnie! Did I hear right? You call Dad a kid?" He laughs at the small white-haired Scotswoman and kisses her head.

"Not just him, you too! If you were also counted correctly, mi amor!" Amused, Rosalía takes the glass from Linda, lifts it in the air and drinks it all in one go. "Lo siento, Linda guapa, but that's what I needed just now! I'm going to get us more of this stuff, even though I can already feel how my poor head will suffer tomorrow! That flight really tried my patience and my nerves!" Then, addressing Ken, she says, "You owe this Señora a lot here! A WHOLE LOT!!!" Theatrically, she lifts her face in the air, tightens her back, pushes her breasts forward and goes into the next room with the empty glass.

"Uh, oh, Ken! It seems to me that Rosalía has maintained her Hispanic temperament very well over all these years." Linda laughs cheerfully as she watches her sweet friend leave the room.

"You can say that again! But that's what I love about her! We all do, right? At least her self-talk has decreased a little since the boys have started talking and she has noticed that they tell her everything! This has led to unpleasant situations here and there." All three burst into loud laughter as Rosa returns with two filled champagne glasses.

"I'm warning you, if you laugh at me, then I'll make chili out of you! I just learned how to do it again! So I'm up to date and very much in top shape!" She hands a glass to Linda and sits next to her again. "So, you were just about to explain to me how everything is so perfect with you!"

Chapter 18

Hailey hangs the carefully ironed shirt on the wooden hanger and heads over to the closet. She glances quickly through the window as she passes it. As if she cannot believe her eyes, she stops and takes a step back, looking out of the window again in surprise. Her face brightens abruptly, and her smile widens the longer she looks out. "My good boy! Just look at how great you look! Hailey knows for sure that you are not the dumb, reckless gray vulture you always pretend to be. I know you too well. Since you first saw the light of this world. And now, finally, you have become a man! Although, it took too long in my opinion. Better the right thing too late than the wrong thing too early."

Hailey does the rest of the laundry a little faster than usual and goes down to the kitchen. A scrutinizing look in the fridge gives her ideas for a tasty meal in the cozy dining room. She takes her jacket from the hook, slips her feet out of her warm slippers and directly into her cold boots. The door is difficult to open, but she soon walks in short but quick steps over to the paddock. "My dear! How nice to have you with us! Welcome!" She extends her hand to Stacy in greeting and takes the woman's right hand in both of her.

"Miss Burns, it's so nice to see you again as well! Your yard is impressive! And I dare say that in my entire life I have never seen such beautiful and well-trained horses! I'm absolutely speechless!" The veterinarian smiles happily at Hailey and blinks, a bit embarrassed, at Angus, who is casually leaning against the fence, one leg propped up.

"Oh, I really hope you'll stay for dinner, I'm sure you don't eat anything decent all alone in your little flat. I would also like to show you the house, a family residence that has existed for centuries. Angus, isn't it true? We would love to have her company, right?!"

Just at that moment, Sam loses focus for an instant and the mare gets away from him. She runs like a fox being hunted over to the other side and starts trotting back and forth along the high fence.

"Damn it, Sam! Never let her out of your sight! She has just crowned herself queen!" Annoyed, he jumps over the fence in the paddock and throws a few final words over his shoulders. "Chatter belongs in the chicken coop!"

Chapter 19

The chairs at the large and elegant wooden table are all occupied, except for the last one. Four beautiful candlesticks, decorative fresh roses and crystal balls are carefully arranged on the table. The white china plates, polished silver cutlery and crystal goblets complete the inviting picture perfectly. Bonnie brings one steaming plate after the other into the room and places them purposefully on the table. All eyes are focused hungrily on the delicious dishes. Rosalía comments, "Oh Bonnie, green beans... homemade mashed potatoes... cranberry jelly... Mmm!!! And what do you have in here? Chicos! Have you ever seen such a feast? Your mamá can't cook like this! So make sure you enjoy every bite today!"

Everyone at the table laughs and Ken puts his arm around her shoulder. "Don't worry, Guapa, you have other good qualities!" He kisses her on the temple and looks at his twins proudly. "Right, guys? No mom can give a massage as well as yours!" In a flash, Rosalía slaps his thigh, saying "I see, you apparently missed my punches too!"

"Well, I would rather be massaged by the big person back there behind the table!" All eyes look at the person who is now standing in the door frame.

"Tia Susie!!!" Shrieking, the identical twins jump up from their chairs and run towards the plump lady.

"Don't knock me down, guys! Tia Susie won't be able to get up if you do!" Susan Manders lets the two boys cuddle up to her and hugs them heartily! "What do they feed you in the South? Wax beans? Man, soon you'll have to carry me on a litter away from the table!" She laughs out loud and pinches the two boys' little arms, covered in bits of mashed potatoes.

"Come, that's your place! Baba said today's lady of the house is Tia Susie!" The two boys take her by the hand and pull her over to the table. Stirred by this reunion and what the children have said, Susie looks at Frank with tears in her eyes and blows him a kiss. She blows more kisses to everyone else in turn until she sees a person who is a stranger to her.

In the meantime, Rosalía has stepped over beside her and, pushing her heartily from the side, says, "Tia Susie, I would like to introduce someone to you." She takes Susie by the elbow and leads her around the table. The woman then gets up from her chair. "This is Mima, my mother, Carmen. Mima, this is our Tia Susie." The two women look at each other for a fraction of a second and hug each other as heartily as if they had waited a long time for this moment.

Chapter 20

In a fresh mood, Hailey busies herself in her kitchen, humming cheerful Scottish songs to herself. She takes the carefully folded tablecloth and the cloth napkins from a drawer. As she starts to walk to the dining room, the phone is ringing. She puts everything aside, smooths her apron as usual and lifts the receiver off the old phone on the kitchen wall. "This is Hailey Burns." Multitasking as always, Hailey grabs the corner of her apron and starts polishing a fork while she listens.

"Excuse me? Who is it? Could you please speak a little louder? My hearing is showing its age." As she speaks, her voice sounding a bit amused, she presses the phone tighter to her ear. "Oh... oh... My boy! Hello! Oh... How nice to hear your wonderful voice! How are you? When are you coming?! How long are you going to make me wait?" She now holds the receiver with both hands and concentrates on the person at the other end.

***

"Hailey!? Hailey?! We're riding to the cliff and we'll be back in an hour!" Angus yells these words out loud through the open front door, waits a moment, and then shrugs the door shut again. "Is everything okay?" Stacy asks him as she looks down at him from the horse and pats the brown gelding's strong neck. "I think so. She probably heard me."

"We're off to the cliffs, then! Wonderful, they must be breathtaking. I have seen so many pictures. Thank you, Angus, for taking the time, despite the chicken chatter!" Amused and yet embarrassed, Stacy squints at the horse and then at her companion.

***

"Did you hear that?! Did you just hear that?!" Hailey slaps a hand over her mouth and her eyes fill with tears of joy. "This is my absolute luckiest day! All my prayers have been answered at once! What a miracle!" She nods her head as if the gesture can be seen through the phone. "Yes, he was! And imagine, he's out riding with a wonderful, oh so wonderful young lady! She is a veterinarian from Glasgow. But now she's here in the north for some study or something. We went out to eat with her today. You should have seen Angus. Terrible, I tell you! You know how he is. But no matter, now she has come and..." She is interrupted, then she replies, "Oh, of course, my boy, what did you want to ask me, Kenneth?"

Chapter 21

The large, graceful, now very cozy house in the Hamptons is filled with hearty laughter and cheerfulness. The delighted bilingual children's voices bring new life to the otherwise extremely calm atmosphere and Frank looks contentedly around his living room. Everyone has chosen a suitable place to give their stuffed bellies a little rest. Of course, the two smallest ones in the family don't need to rest.

They run up the spiral staircase and screech as they race down from the landing again.

"Díos mío!!! Boys!!! Stop it IMMEDIATELY or Mamá will make burritos out of you! Did you hear me?!" Rosalía throws both hands in the air and then puts them around her narrow waist and continues "I am warning you for the last time!!!" She continues cursing in Spanish as Linda sits next to her, holding a cup of hot tea in her hand.

"Should I put some water on to boil for you or are your threats as full of lies as mine have always been?" She holds out the cup to the small Mexican woman and watches the wild boys standing up on the landing, both of them grinning.

"Linda, díme, how is Roberto really? Why is he still sitting in that awful chair?!" Rosa turns demonstratively and shows her back to the two savages. Linda looks at her and sighs deeply, "Rosa, you have to speak plainly to him! You would not believe how stubborn he is! He won't listen to me – what do I know about medicine?" She rolls her eyes and stares at the boys standing on the landing. "Hey, boys! Don't you want to do a round with Uncle Roberto? I'm sure he has missed that!" She claps her hands encouragingly and leads them into the living room.

With determined steps, the former physiotherapist follows Linda and her wild brood into the living room and guides them over to where Roberto is sitting. "But only one round for each of you, and then it's Mamá's turn!" She draws an imaginary circle in the air and winks at Roberto, who takes the first twin on his lap and skillfully steers his wheelchair past Rosa. "I'm sorry, Señora, you should have come up with this idea at the clinic back then. Now I have my wife again and you got that Scottish lawyer! Hasta luego!" He disappears into the adjoining room and her son's happy shriek sounds like a violin playing in Rosalía's ear. Her gaze wanders over to Linda, who has returned to the other room in the meantime and is now sitting with Frank and Ken. Rosalía murmurs, "Your wife is back, yes... But we have not yet reached our goal, Señor Doctor!"

Chapter 22

Silently, the two strangers ride side by side through the picturesque highlands of Scotland. Although Angus knows every stone, every tree, and every sand hill, he still repeatedly loses himself in his thoughts, inspired by the peace and security that this land instills in him. A country, his country, which he could never leave and therefore never will leave. He still often asks himself how his sister was so easily capable of leaving everything behind. This greed of humanity, to want to own everything. Be famous and rich. To see everything in the world and experience everything. What for? In the end, everyone is simply a pale body inside a box under the ground or a pile of burned ashes inside a small pot. What is the point of it all? Why can't people enjoy what they have? Be thankful for every day that your lungs fill with air, your heart diligently organizes your blood in your body and your mind plays no tricks on you?

"Angus?" The hesitant female voice next to him interrupts his recurrent musing on the philosophy of life. Does she also ask herself such questions? Maybe he would ask her about all this. Yes, maybe he would do that. And if she is really as great as Hailey claims, perhaps she will even have an answer or two. He looks at her without replying because he feels a clumsy "Yes" would be out of place when he looks at her. It appears as if she has guessed his thought correctly and she gives him a smile. "May I ask you something or would you rather continue pondering?" His frown and his pursed lips tell her that she caught him in the act. He blinks, slightly embarrassed, clears his throat and tightens the reins of his stallion. He looks calmly down the path and replies, "You can always ask questions if you won't shy away from the answer. At least, that's what my old master taught me before he drank himself to death."

Since this has already been a bit too much conversation for him, he gives his horse a gentle kick and clicks his tongue. Stacy does the same in a flash and they gallop up to the top of the cliff, where they give the snorting animals a rest. They stand side by side and look out over the wild sea.

"Are those the Orkney Islands?" Stacy points her finger in the direction of the mainland. "Aye" is the answer she receives in reply, and she smiles. "I read in a book that these islands are supposed to be haunted. Do you know more about this myth?" She seems to have aroused his interest because he settles more comfortably on the saddle and looks toward the islands. "It would be better if you asked Hailey. She knows all the ghost stories from all over Scotland and she's a fantastic storyteller!" Surprised by his own answer, he looks at his horse with an expression of irritation on his face and pats him on his strong neck.

"That's great! I will definitely do that. I love to listen to stories!"

"Then wait and see what Hailey knows about our family! Or have you already heard the flowery village gossip?"

Chapter 23

"Mirjam, do you want to take these little chili peppers to bed? I think the champagne, wine and whisky have done a number on me and I am no longer capable of telling a bedtime story." Kenneth holds each of his children by the hand and looks questioningly at the girl sitting on Frank's lap.

"Of course! Come on, boys, I'll tell you the story of the pirate with just one eye!" Joyful screeching echoes throughout the house and the youngest generation heads towards the guest house. As soon as the silence returns, Susie breaks it. "Well, and now out with it. What happens now? I mean, something has to happen here, right? When and where is it happening?!" With a curious expression, she looks from one face to the other and Roberto decides to speak. "I have good news!" He takes Linda's hand, who is standing next to him, and continues, "We have a specialist who will see Carmen. And this week, already!"

A glass falls to the ground and crystal splinters. "Caramba!!! Díos mío!!! Holy Mother! Roberto!!! Mummy! Ken!" Rosalía screeches these exclamations one after the other from behind her hand that she's holding in front of her mouth and does not know whom to address first. Frank laughs, slaps his thighs and starts to stand up as Bonnie rushes over to Rosa, holding a broom. "Do not move, my dear!"

"I'm sorry Frank, Bonnie!! I... I'll replace the glass for you... But,.. But, did you hear that?! Roberto! Who? Where? And how did this happen?!" Despite Bonnie's warning, she approaches her mother, who is still completely unaware of what's going on, but visibly confused. She is sitting next to Susie on the leather couch and she looks inquiringly into her daughter's beautiful eyes, holding both her hands tightly. "Qué pasa, guapa? Todo bien?" Her barely intelligible sounds only make sense to Rosalía.

"Oh, Mima!!! Roberto has found you one of the best specialists and he wants to see you! Mamá, do you know what that means?!" She takes her mother's face between her hands and kisses her on both cheeks. The person in question seems to understand very well and her eyes fill with tears. She holds her hands tightly to her face and nods. She tears herself away from her daughter's trembling hands and starts speaking in sign language. Rosa answers her excitedly and vigorously shakes her head.

64

"Oh, oh... But this looks like a family quarrel! How does this happen? From one second to the other? What are they arguing about now, Ken?" Frank looks amazed and surprised from the two silently arguing women to his son, who leans against the door frame, smiling. He swirls the golden elixir in his glass and answers, "I will not answer this question, but another question you asked me today. No, Dad, they'll probably never get used to being part of the MacKay clan and bearing the name Conley."

Chapter 24

"Angus!? Where are you?! I always have to search for you!" Hailey stomps excitedly through the stable and turns around again. She walks across the gravel yard and sees the tall man coming out of the horse stalls. She hasn't reached him yet and she keeps yelling, "Where is she?! What did you do with Stacy?!" She looks past him, confused. When she doesn't see anyone else, she stands demonstratively in front of her protégé and raises her forefinger. "Immediately, Angus, tell me where our visitor is!"

"By the cliffs. Shall I saddle a horse for you?" He reluctantly puts both hands in his trouser pockets and rocks back and forth on his heels.

"By the cliffs?! Have you been abandoned by all the good spirits?! Why did you leave her alone by the cliffs?! Well... I... I cannot believe it! Angus Cunningham MacKay, you're probably the most horrible and mean and... and..." She turns furiously, snorting and raging toward the house, but then hears a lovely woman's voice addressing her. "Miss Burns, are you alright?" In a flash, the small furious woman turns on her heels and looks in astonishment into Stacy's big eyes, who is now approaching them. "Has something happened?" The visitor from the MacKay yard looks first at Hailey, then at Angus and then back again.

"Oh my dear! You are here! But... I do not understand... Where were you?"

"Angus was kind enough to let me use the bathroom. I should not have drunk so much before riding. I'm sorry, I didn't know that was why I'm causing a stir."

"You?! Causing a stir?!" Hailey has no idea what to do. She would like to grab the dolt by the throat. "Angus, I'm speechless! Where are your manners?! You're kidding me! I'm so sorry Stacy. I apologize for this lout! How dare he let you use the nasty stall toilet. You must have a terrible impression of us!" She takes Stacy by the hand and throws a scathing glance at the mischievously grinning farm owner. "Come, my dear, we'll go into the house. You can freshen up in the nice bathroom."

As they are about to enter the house, Hailey looks back and shouts at Angus, "And I'll meet you in the kitchen! There is a change in plans! Kenneth called."

Chapter 25

After the heated tempers finish calming down, Susie accompanies the silent Carmen to the guesthouse. She feels guilty about having messed things up so badly and can clearly understand why the anxious woman does not want to be dependent on others. The good-hearted receptionist from Coney

Island Hospital knows very well what it felt like to be involved with the Conleys in the beginning. It is a different world and it will always be that way for her. Even though she now holds everyone here so tightly in her heart, she will always enjoy heading back to her small, run-down house, putting on her old Walmart housecoat and slipping into her pink plush sandals. But this new thing here is something else, and she will have to teach Carmen! This is about a miracle produced by today's medicine! To bring back someone's hearing when everyone thought it was lost forever. What must be, must be!

***

Soft piano sounds can be heard in the large living room, magically attracting all the guests. Rosalía sits on Ken's lap, who has made himself comfortable in a chair. Susie and Bonnie sit next to Frank on the long sofa and Linda lies back on the chaise longue. She closes her eyes and is carried away by Roberto's dexterity on the fly. Silent tears roll down her cheeks. Roberto displays his talent as he plays the white and black keys, a wistful smile on his face as he skillfully operates the pedals. Rosalía looks at her husband, kisses him tenderly and whispers something in his ear. His gaze wanders to Roberto's foot on the pedals and replicates Rosa's nod. Frank swirls the whisky in his glass, squeezes Bonnie tightly with his other arm and lets his thoughts wander off into the distance.

"That was beautiful, as usual, Bob!" Rosa frees herself from Ken's arms and approaches the big man sitting at the piano, putting her hand on his shoulder and bending over to his ear, "I know you can move your legs... What's the drama with the wheelchair about?" They exchange glances and Roberto replies, "It's not quite as easy as you think, Rosa. But let's not talk about it now, ok?"

"What are you two whispering about again? These healthcare people – they're always discussing something together!" Susan Manders gets up from the sofa, straightens her cardigan and secretly enjoys the weight she has lost. She walks over to Linda with a smile. Linda is still lying on the chaise longue, blowing her nose. "What is happening, sweetie?" Susie sits down at the foot of the chaise longue and grabs one of her young friend's ankles. "Nothing actually. It's always the same. And as soon as I hear his piano playing, I'm thrown back into all those awful memories, you know!" She pulls her legs sideways and looks over at Frank.

"There's something else I have to tell you..." Conley Senior sits at the edge of the sofa, takes his glass in both hands and looks into it thoughtfully. "When I picked up Mirjam from school today, they were right in the middle of an experiment." He looks with raised eyebrows first at Roberto, then at Linda and Susie. "I think it's time..." He bites his lower lip and wrinkles his forehead. "They have figured out their blood types and are supposed to then evaluate those of their parents...!"

Chapter 26

With short steps, Hailey enters her large kitchen, where, as usual, it smells heavenly. Angus closes the refrigerator, removes the cap from the beer bottle and throws it into the sink. At the same time, Hailey snorts loudly and starts to comment on something as he takes the cap out of the sink and throws it into the trash can standing next to him. The small Scotswoman takes a deep breath, shakes her head slightly and goes over to the oven. She opens it and casts a searching glance in. "Very nice, it will be done soon. Stacy is freshening up. I lent her some clothes, so she won't smell like horse stalls at the table." She turns on her heels and points with a wooden spoon towards the tall man standing in her kitchen." And you, my dear, I advise you to do the same! I do not want to smell horse dung when I serve this heavenly roast! And you must put on some decent clothes!"

"Understood, m'lady! And also fresh underwear! These things will slowly wear out if I have to change them all the time!" Angus grins mischievously, takes another sip from the bottle of beer and sits down on one of the chairs. "What does Ken say?" He looks out the window into the garden and lets his tongue slide over his lower lip.

"Oh Angus!!!" She walks over to him and stops right in front of him, so he's forced to look at her. Tall and short allow them to meet eye to eye. "Well, there is something that I have not told you about Kenneth... Well, um... they will not all be coming..."

Angus' face appears to brighten, but he answers calmly. "Good! Much better that way! I would have buried that monster alive in the horse manure anyway!"

"How can you even think of anything so horrible!" Hailey crosses herself and holds both fists on the waist. "He's part of your, our family! How much longer do you want to twist the truth and grieve? And whether you like it or not, he is always welcome here in my home! Just like everyone else!"

She stomps over to the oven, turns the heat on and gets to work on the pots. She realizes that Angus has risen and is now standing close behind her. She has to go out of her way to ignore him because she can't find the words to tell him how many guest rooms she will actually be getting ready.

Chapter 27

Linda paces excitedly back and forth in the room. Again and again she stops, looks into the darkness behind the glass in the window and looks at her own reflection in it. "She will not be able to understand it yet! She is still too young for that. Roberto, we urgently need to talk to the teacher! He will find a way." She turns and looks at her husband, who is still sitting at the piano. Lost in thought, he slides his forefinger over the keys and taps the highest, last note pointedly. "No, we knew this day would come and now it's here! Mirjam is a very smart and sensible girl. She will cope with it. Everything takes time and we will give it to her. We needed time as well."

"I agree with Roberto. You, we should tell her. Bring her in the loop, get her involved." Frank gets up from the sofa and walks over to Linda. "I understand your concerns, Linda, but remember what we, you had to go through and what you are still reminded of every day. What happened to Roberto and what stories we have all had to tell each other. Isn't it now time to take further steps? We have never given up hope and now we are being given another chance!"

"I will take Mirjam to the office tomorrow and show her everything..." Roberto starts to move away from the piano as he is held back by Rosalía. "I can accompany you both if you allow me." She looks from him to Linda, who looks out the window again.

"I cannot go with you, Habibi! I cannot do it... I'm so sorry... But I simply cannot do it!" Sad and thoughtful, Linda imperceptibly shakes her head.

"It's alright, you don't have to apologize. I am not the only one responsible – I also have to accept the consequences. You have already made too many sacrifices. Mirjam will seek comfort from you." Roberto rolls his wheelchair next to her and takes her sweaty cold hand in his.

Chapter 28

"Ohh, my dear, you look very pretty in that dress! I knew you were the same size as me!" Hailey walks over to the woman in the romantic flowery dress, who is standing in the open doorway, and holds her arms out to her. "Thank you, Miss Burns, it's really a pretty dress." She smoothes the plush fabric over her body with both hands. "I've never worn such a dress before." Embarrassed, she looks at Angus, who is kneeling by the fireplace, getting a fire started.

"No wonder, it was before you were born when the women here wore those kinds of clothes." He puts a new piece of wood on the flames and closes the fireplace glass.

"Angus, please! Where are your manners? That's not how you compliment someone! She looks so pretty!"

"Excuse me, ma'am, you look gorgeous! May I offer you something to drink?" He walks over to the window with a grin on his face. In front of the window, there is a side table with various bottles, glasses and decanters on top of it. As if he were presenting the entire sky to her, he holds his outstretched arm in front of it.

"Thank you so much for this lovely compliment, sir!" Stacy skillfully plays along with the charade and does a little kick as she gently lifts her gown with her fingertips. Hailey, who is clearly delighted, claps her hands over her mouth and makes a rapturous sound. Before she lets the tears spring to her eyes, she quickly turns around and walks into the kitchen.

"Oh, I hope that was not too much?" Stacy looks after her with a worried look on her face.

"Au contraire! That was the cherry on top of the ice cream!" Angus opens a black bottle with golden contents and pours some of it into two crystal glasses. He picks them both up and walks toward his flowery guest. "Here, this is distilled on Orkney Island, Highland Park Distillery. Those are some crazy Vikings over there, but they make damned good whisky." He hands her a glass and winks at her.

"Are you flirting with me?" Stacy accepts the glass with a smile and walks over to the cozy armchair next to the fire. She is just about to sit down when she is verbally held back by her host. "No flower dresses can sit in that chair. It's only for leather-clad men's bottoms." He poses next to her demonstratively. Contrary to his expectations, she sits down with great pleasure, caresses the arm of the chair, and takes a sniff of her whisky. "Well then, on to new traditions!" She takes a big swallow, emptying the glass, and says in a deep voice, "Praise to the Vikings!" His mouth open and a perplexed look in his eyes, Angus stares at the woman sitting in his chair. He blinks his amazement away quickly and takes her glass. "Look here! We have a booze hound in the house! I assume Madame would like a refill?!" Without waiting for an answer, he goes over to the whisky bottles and pours again.

"Speaking of animals! You were right – the village sparrows have been chirping quite a bit all day long. Why don't you tell me your version of the MacKay family saga? Who is Kenneth, for example?"

Chapter 29

The large, light-colored wooden table and the matching chairs with colorful cushions in the breakfast room send out an inviting, seductive fragrance in the air. As the first to arrive, Frank sits at the head of the table, a newspaper in one hand and a steaming teacup in the other. Kenneth goes into the kitchen and over to Bonnie first, hugs her from the side and kisses her on the head. "Good morning, Bonnie. Did you work through the entire night? It smells wonderful! What would we do without you?" He then goes through the open kitchen to the large, stylishly laid table and sits down at the opposite end from Frank.

"I know what I would do at least NOW without Bonnie." Conley Senior puts his teacup on the table, wrinkles his nose, and folds up the newspaper purposefully, continuing, "I would drink a strong, home-brewed, Italian espresso! Yes, did you hear, Bonnie? That is what I would do!" He lifts his cup again, sniffs the dark liquid and makes a disgusted sound. He looks around the table and seems to have found a way out. "Good morning to you too, my boy! What do you think? Are your boys thirsty?" He winks at Ken and reaches for a children's cup, filled with hot chocolate, at the place next to him.

One sleepy face after the other joins the two Conleys. Rosalía, followed by her two little pajama wearers, take the last places at the table.

"Mirjam, I heard from Skipper that you're analyzing your blood at school. What do you think about going to my office with Rosa and doing it together? I would like to show you and explain a little more." Roberto takes a leisurely bite of his still warm croissant and looks at his daughter questioningly. She stirs her cereal slowly and dreamily, and murmurs, "Hmm... I don't know, Dad. Weren't we all going to do something together?" She raises her shoulders and looks first at the twins, then at her father. But before he can reply, Rosalía intervenes and says with a slightly exaggerated tone, "Por favor, mi querida! Mamá needs to do something new once in a while and get away from these chili peppers here! Por favor!" She folds her hands in prayer and blinks at Mirjam pleadingly.

Mirjam giggles to herself and says, "Okay, if that will do you some good! But I will do the blood test at school anyway. You know, Dad, no one has had such an exotic mix yet! And it will be great, as dark as I am, with you as parents! Nobody believes me still!"

Chapter 30

With a beaming expression on her face, Hailey pushes a serving trolley into the dining room. Through the open archway, she looks nervously into the living room and frowns in confusion. "What's going on here?! Are you not feeling well, Stacy?! Angus?! What have you done?!" She walks quickly over to the visitor, who appears to be lost in thought, and looks at her questioningly, "My dear, you look like you've seen a ghost?!"

"And she did!" Angus gets up from a leather armchair with an empty glass in his hand and walks past the two women, taking the empty glass from the pale guest. "It's on the house today." And once he's standing by the whisky bar, he adds, "Welcome to MacKay, the horror seat of all the Highland clans." He pours the golden liquid into both glasses and corks the bottle.

"My dear, what did he tell you?! You must not believe everything he says! He always exaggerates enormously and then his imagination gets the better of him until there is no end to it! Come on, the food is ready. It will do you good!" Hailey pats Stacy on the shoulders and gives Angus a withering look. He innocently raises his shoulders and defends himself, saying, "She asked, and I was polite, as you always expect me to be, and I gave her an answer. Not my fault we are not a picture-book clan!" He walks past the small Scotswoman and stands in front of the young woman, who is still sitting. He reaches out to hand her the glass and waves it slightly in front of her face. "Here, for you! You really have lost some color in your face. And I was not even finished." He grins slightly as her long-fingered, cold hands reach for the glass.

"You're impossible, Angus, no, really! I can't even leave you alone with a guest for five minutes! I am truly sorry, my dear! Please excuse his behavior! It's just that he's always alone with me here and..." She hasn't finished her apologetic plea when Stacy interrupts her. "It's alright, Miss Burns. Angus didn't do or say anything wrong... It was... Well, to put it more clearly, it is more that..."

A loud knock on the large wooden door interrupts their conversation. The knocking gets more powerful and louder, followed by a deep male voice, saying, "Damned son of a bitch, get your rich ass out here immediately!!! I know what you're planning on doing!!! Come out, I know you're in there!!!"

Chapter 31

As if they are on a secret mission, the three adventurers get out of the black limousine and walk over to the glass front door. Rosalía looks up at the modern building and shakes her head slightly. "Caramba! It's amazing how huge the differences are. Not even three hours of flight and you are in a totally different world. And I will never belong here!" Mirjam holds open the big door for her father and asks, "What do you mean, Tia Rosa?"

Her aunt goes over to the teenage girl, puts her arm around her and hugs her close. "I'll explain that to you another time, querida! Now we have an exciting trip ahead of us. Rápido, you know how impatient your father can be! Oooh... Santo Domingo! He almost drove me crazy as a patient! Now look at him, Señor Doctor! A private doctor's office as a general practitioner! Did you actually check his papers? Did he really graduate from university or just fake the papers?" The cheerful Latina woman winks amused at her still ignorant compatriot.

"Don't listen to her, sweetie! I was her favorite patient of all time!" Roberto confirms for his daughter, using their mother tongue. This makes her entire face glow with happiness.

"What did he say? Qué dijo? Hey amigo! This violates the family rules! No secret languages if not everyone can understand it! And I am present, and I can't understand your 'chchch' Swiss language! What did he say, querida?"

"But you can use your Mexican swear words and phrases wherever and whenever you want?" Roberto laughs out loud and stops in the open elevator door so the two women can slip past him.

83

"Spanish is not a secret language! But your alpine language makes no sense!" Rosa wrinkles her nose and sticks the tip of her tongue out of her mouth. Mirjam and Roberto laugh, happy to have their heartfelt friend with them again. The past weeks without the children and Rosalía have not been the same. Mirjam cuddles with the former physiotherapist.

"He said he was your favorite patient." She looks her in the eye and notices the smile on Rosa's lips, who says, "And he isn't lying, he really was! It's unimaginable where I would be today if I had never met your father."

Roberto gives her a smile as well and then looks at Mirjam. "That goes for all of us, Rosa..."

Chapter 32

With helpless, expectant looks, the two women sit at the richly set table in the rustic dining room. Hailey has her elbows propped on the table and keeps her hands folded as if in prayer. Stacy watches the lady of the house and has no idea if she should address her or wait a moment. This inexplicable situation, Angus' story, and the fact that she is in this house with apparently questionable strangers, all seem to worry her more than she would have thought possible. As if the elderly lady can hear her thoughts, she gently addresses her, "You needn't worry, dear. Angus will be back soon and then we will enjoy the food. I should warm it up. Cold food does not taste good! How stupid of me, that I didn't think of it sooner!" She starts to get up when Stacy puts her hand on hers. "Miss Burns... What's going on here?! Who was that?!" She looks questioningly at the now very sad looking woman sitting across from her at the table.

"My dear, it's such a horrible and cruel story... And the food has gotten cold and Angus is still out and..." Confused, Hailey looks from Stacy to the dinner on the table and then out the window into the darkness. "You must understand, he's such a good boy! It's just that he has such a terribly hard shell, but deep down in his heart he's a loving, kind and gentle boy... Man... My Angus... He didn't have it easy, do

85

you understand, my dear? He really did not have it easy..." Her tears softly roll down her pale, wrinkled face. She takes a handkerchief from her sweater sleeve and wipes her nose. Carefully, she folds it up and puts it back. She pats Stacy's hand and looks at her sadly.

She starts to open her mouth again when the heavy front door slams open in the other room. Both women look up and wait for the arrival of the host. They hear his heavy boots stomping through the entryway and then see him shortly thereafter standing in the passageway.

"You are still here? Shall I drive you back to the village? I assume you have heard and seen enough?" He puts his hands in his trouser pockets and leans against the wooden posts. His gaze reveals no emotions. Stacy's look of astonishment slowly morphs into a grin. She stretches back into her chair and announces, "On the contrary! Now that everything seems to have been clarified, we shouldn't wait any longer to eat this delicious meal prepared meal by Miss Burns, right?!"

Chapter 33

Roberto moves his wheelchair closer to the table in front of them and takes the tray with all the utensils from his lap. Carefully he places it on the clean tabletop and points to the opposite side of the room. "Sweetie, please bring the microscope over here so I don't have to drive around with the blood."

"What, if you walk with it instead, Roberto! Get up and use your legs!" Rosalía demonstratively stands next to him and puts both hands on her hips. "Come on, I'll help you stand up. No better opportunity than this one. Who else can say they have their own personal physical therapist all to themselves, and at no cost!?" She winks at the astonished Mirjam and waits for Mirjam's father's answer.

"Not now, Rosa, we need to concentrate on this!" He draws circles with his finger over the utensils in front of him.

As Mirjam notices that no attempts to walk will be made, she continues, grabs the microscope and carefully places it on the table, before returning to the seat beside her father.

"You Americans sit far too often! Caramba! We are equipped with two magnificent legs, a strong back and incredible rump muscles. But no, instead of keeping everything healthy, you neglect these wonderful gifts and flatten your butt!" The small, fit physiotherapist throws her hands over her head and remains standing between the two.

"You're right, Tia Rosa, and I'm still young, after all!" Mirjam gets up, puts the stool aside and stands next to Rosalía. Both of them look at the tall man in the wheelchair, who shrugs his shoulders in amusement. "It's my own fault. This will take a long time to fix! Can physiotherapists also withdraw blood or just rush their patients around the room?" He gives Rosa a questioning smile and holds out a package containing a straight pin. Eyebrows raised, she takes this from him and opens the plastic of the package. "I could, if I wanted to, but I won't. And since I'm actually a guest in this family doctor's office, I'm allowed to go first. Let's see where my ancestors hung around... to say it literally!" She chuckles to herself, dabbing her fingertip and giving herself a quick prick. Carefully, she squeezes a few drops onto the glass slide and immediately covers it with a second one. She gives Roberto a questioning look as she hands it to Mirjam. He takes this as a sign that his companion now considers this a convenient time to come out with the truth.

Chapter 34

As they eat, Stacy steals a few wondering glances at her host. Who was that raging man at the door and how could she find out in a courteous manner? She lifts another forkful of vegetables from her plate and gives Hailey an admirable smile. "How do you manage it, Miss Burns? No matter what I eat, every bite tastes just heavenly! I am not lying or exaggerating when I say that I have never had such a delicious meal in my entire life! And the worst part is that I've been full for quite a while now. I can barely get up from my chair." She laughs and opens her mouth to eat the forkful of vegetables. The cook gives her a grateful smile and pats her hand. "It's nice that it tastes so good, my dear! You are always welcome at our table, right, Angus?" She looks at the Scotsman as he chews his food and lets out a thoughtful mumble.

"Oh, thank you very much! Of course I accept your offer! Even, if I will have to go up a dress size soon!" She pats her stomach and tries to lighten the mood at the table. Angus gives her a scrutinizing look, which he then immediately turns to his plate, saying, "It wouldn't hurt for you to gain a few pounds!" Grinning, he puts a piece of meat in his mouth, curious to see what will happen.

"Angus!? What are you thinking, speaking like that to our guest! You don't say things like that to a lady!" Hailey gives him an angry look and immediately starts to apologize to Stacy, who laughs in amusement, saying, "It's alright, it's alright, I take that as a compliment. I'm glad to hear that a bit of plumpness in women is still in style today. And if I'm going to help him with the horses, then I really need more energy. They are not only beautiful, but also very strong animals, right, Mr. MacKay?" She raises a provocative eyebrow and looks forward to his reaction to this challenge. Angus looks at her blankly, then over at Hailey, and grabs the bowl with the still warm mashed potatoes. He places it noisily in front of Stacy and hands her the ladle. "That's absolutely correct! And how those critters can shit! That's really hard to shovel away, I can tell you! You're always welcome to help out, m'lady!" He lowers his head as if he has just been knighted.

"Hm, amazing... Truly amazing..." Stacy calmly takes the ladle being held out to her, spoons another pile of the mashed potatoes and casually sighs, "How right Heather was..."

Chapter 35

Eyes huge and mouth open, Mirjam looks first at her father, then at Rosalía. Slowly she takes her seat and begins to tremble. The thick silence is broken by Rosalía's movement to touch Mirjam's fragile hands. The confused girl looks searchingly at her aunt and begins to sob, "You all knew about this... all of you lied to me the entire time... I don't understand... Why... I... But who?!..." Her initial sadness begins turning to rage and her gaze becomes piercing and demanding. Her lips tremble and she rises from her stool.

"Who are my real parents?! Why did they give me away? Why you?! Where are they? Still in Mexico? You knew all along and never told me?!" She throws a devastating look at the two messengers and grabs the microscope. "And this alibi exercise here?! That was your great idea to show meh that I'm not your flesh and blood? We could have spared ourselves the trip here or was Mama too cowardly to say it to my face?! And Skipper! And Susie! All too cowardly!" She begins to heave the microscope across the room, but her father is too quick. In a single bound, Roberto leaps from his wheelchair, grabs hold of the instrument with one hand and cradles his daughter's head with the other. Rosa quickly takes the microscope from his hand, leaving him a free to take Mirjam in his arms. The now crying girl collapses in his embrace, sobbing loudly.

"Shh... It's all right... I know it hurts... And I'm so sorry, my sweet... But there is never an appropriate moment for a revelation like this... Shh...!"

The tall doctor stands shakily on both legs, holding his daughter in his arms, laying his chin on her head and fighting back his own tears. Rosalía watches the two with compassion. She takes a step forward and lays a comforting hand on Mirjam's back. "Mi querida, this whole story is so deeply engrained in all of our bones that none of us could bear any more suffering. And you... Yes, YOU were the single bright star in this dark sky. Only because of YOU have we all come together into a big, loving family! Without you, none of this would be here!" Rosa brings her gaze back up. "I would not be a wife, a mama. Skipper would not be a proud grandfather and your mama and your papa... I cannot even imagine what would have become of them by now if they had not received YOU as a gift!"

She has barely finished saying these words when the silenced girl breaks away from the embrace and looks at her with fury saying, "Exactly, a worthless gift! Like a forgotten, exchanged and unloved object, I was given away! Just given to strangers, like...like...!" She looks around the room desperately, as if she could find the word somewhere in it.

"Like the greatest, most wonderful and perfect gift ever made! And you're still that, Mirjam!" Roberto looks tenderly at the desperate girl, who returns his gaze with visible disappointment. Mirjam frowns and folds her arms across her chest.

"How long have you known?"

Chapter 36

The surprised faces at the table appear to be sitting tight. With relish, Stacy shoves a fork piled high with food in her mouth and closes her eyes. On the one hand to show again how much she enjoys this meal, and on the other hand to avoid the decision about whose eyes she should look at first. Who would break the ice now? She hears someone clear their throat and is glad that she can open her eyes again without having to stretch out the moment artificially. She looks at Hailey, smiling, and says, "Simply delicious!"

"My dear..., what did you just say?" The petite and delicate Scotswoman looks at her with wide eyes. "Did you mean OUR Heather?" She crosses herself hastily and lays her hand again on Stacy's. Stacy nods, dabs her mouth with the napkins in her other hand, and replies, "May she rest in peace, my beloved Heather." She lays her free hand on Hailey's frail hand and looks at her earnestly. "I did not come by chance this far north to apply my expertise, Miss Burns." Stacy looks into Angus' frowning face and adds, "I wanted to meet you, Angus. Heather talked about you constantly... And those stories were the most beautiful I ever heard throughout my entire childhood..."

"Holy Mother of God, Virgin Mary! My child, what are you talking about? How did you know our Heather? How is that possible?! Angus?! Say something? Can you hear what she is saying!?" The excited Scotswoman can no longer sit quietly. She gets up as fast as her body will allow. With short steps, Hailey rushes around the table and places a hand on the tense shoulders of the silent master of the house. He slowly lays down his cutlery, wordlessly folds his napkin and pushes his chair away from the table. He rises slowly and menacingly, lets his big hands disappear into his trouser pockets and directs his cold gaze to the door.

"I will take care of the horses now. When I get back, I expect to find no liars, parasites or other curious vermin in my house. I think, Hailey, you have understood me unmistakably!" He does not take leave of either of the women present and exits with big, heavy steps.

Chapter 37

Lost in thought, the disappointed and sad teenage girl sips at the glass of water Rosalía has given her. Her red, swollen eyes look down at the floor, her recurring sobs breaking the hearts of those present. "If only Mama had never discovered this stupid liver spot... Then everything would be exactly as it had been an hour ago..." She stomps her foot demonstratively and takes another sip of the soothing cool water.

"I do not think so, my sweet. The liver spot was not good... Who knows what it would have done to your body?" Roberto walks cautiously toward her and tries to hug her again, but his daughter pushes him away. "But... What happened to the other baby? With your baby? Where is she?" She looks hopelessly from her father to Rosalía. These two look at each other and Rosalía starts to talk as she approaches the small pile of misery in the shape of a girl. "Unfortunately, we have not found her yet. When your parents found out they were not your biological parents, they immediately resumed the search... And that was part of the reason why I traveled to Mexico for such a long time. Not only to get Mima, but to find out more about your origins and her disappearance..." She reaches for her handbag on the table and opens it.

"What is this?" Mirjam takes the envelope that is held out to her and opens it slowly. She takes out a folded piece of paper and tries to read it. "What's written here? It's Spanish, right? Rosalía?" Rosa nods and puts her arm around the girl's shoulders. "Yes, mi querida, it's Spanish. That's what I brought back for you from Mexico." She looks at Roberto, who clears his throat and points with his forefinger to a name at the top of the paper, while Mirjam reads aloud, "Valeria Maria Fernando Flores..." She looks sadly at her father and asks in her own native language, "Papa, is that ME?! Is that my real name?!"

Chapter 38

"I have told you clearly, I don't want that person in my house any longer! What is not clear about that?" Furious, Angus stomps through the kitchen and opens the refrigerator to take out some milk for his morning coffee. He closes the door loudly and looks at Hailey, his eyes full of scorn. She calmly stirs a big spoon in her bowl and looks out the window. "I heard you clearly, Angus. I can also hear you very well now, so you don't have to yell." She points with the spoon out the window and nods in the same direction, saying, "She did not sleep in your HOUSE, but in the guest house. There was never any question about that." She lets the spoon rest in the liquid, wipes both of her hands on her lace apron, and turns to face the furious Scotsman, saying, "I'll tell you how this is going to go, my boy! And Hailey will not tolerate any arguments today!" Threateningly, she takes a few steps forward and looks up at him. "I will ask Sam to pick up our guest for breakfast. And you will keep us company and listen to her! I want... I expect... And I would like for you to listen to what she has to say! Do you understand me?!"

***

As he was instructed, Sam, the stable boy, walks with shuffling steps toward the guesthouse to invite the guest to the meal. After repeated knocking with no response, he tries to turn the door knob carefully. The door is unlocked and opens. Sam peaks shyly through the gap. "Ma'am? Hello?! Are you awake? Miss Stacy? Ma'am, is everything okay?" He takes a tentative step into the living room and doesn't hear a sound. After speaking a few more times and ensuring himself that she is not there, he checks all the rooms. In the bedroom, finds an envelope with the inscription "Angus" lying on the neatly made bed. He sticks it in his jacket pocket.

Back at the large house, a seductive scent of fried bacon, sausages, hash browns and fresh waffles penetrates his nose. Sam starts salivating and his stomach begins to make demanding sounds. He takes off his boots and heads towards the fragrance factory. "Sam? Is that you? Stacy, my dear?" Hailey comes out of the kitchen and smiles at the stable boy until she realizes he's alone. She frowns, but before she can ask anything, Sam holds out the envelope to her.

"Yes, but what is this? Where is Stacy?" The only answer she receives is a shoulder shrug. She looks at the envelope and walks into the kitchen. "Come, my boy, you're definitely hungry! Sit down." She shows him a seat at the table covered with plates of delicious food and slams the envelope down noisily onto the table in front of Angus.

"I hope you are satisfied now!"

Chapter 39

Roberto looks out at the busy streets of Brooklyn and listens to the ringing sound in his ear. His eyes wander to the wheelchair in the corner and his lungs fill with air that he inhales deeply. The time has now come in which he must pay attention. The miracle is allowed to happen, and he must preserve an enormous amount of attention that he will need to finally find his daughter, his own flesh and blood. "Hey Habibi, yes we are still in the office. Yes, she knows... As expected... She is very brave; she is a gem... No, not yet. Yes, she gave it to her, and they are already on the Internet... Jasmin, I will leave the wheelchair here... Yes, I am sure... The time has come. Can you please inform Frank and Ken?... Ok... I think we'll go eat something and then come. ... Yes, good, I'll do that... I love you!" Roberto presses a button on the display and puts his cell phone in his pant pocket.

"Who is hungry and in the mood for something enormously unhealthy?" With an encouraging tone, the general practitioner tries to get the attention of the two women sitting in front of the screen. Rosalía looks up and gives him a strange look. "What did Mike say back then about where the bastard wanted to go? Costa Rica?" Mirjam now also looks up and gazes at her father questioningly. He frowns and walks over to the screen. "Yes, he did... Why?"

His daughter turns the screen in his direction so that he can see it clearly. His eyes widen and his mouth opens at the same time. "But... It can't be... How... How did you find that?... Where?... But why did the FBI... I don't understand... What kind of website is that, Mirjam?!" He approaches the screen and grabs it with both hands. The photo staring back, brings tears to Robertos's eyes. His lips begin to tremble, and his eyes narrow to small slits as he lets out a loud scream, grabs the screen off the table with enormous force and throws it through the lovingly furnished reception area of his own doctor's office.

Chapter 40

Speechless and visibly touched, the large Scotsman places the hand-written letter on the table. He inhales through his nose and suppresses the tears that spring to his eyes. Hailey, concerned, walks over and places the plate of steaming hash browns in front of him. She puts her hand comfortingly on his

102

arm and says in a gentle tone, "She wrote it to you, I see. Even if she is a brave girl, you should get her back. She won't have gotten far yet."

The starving stable boy at the other end of the table looks up, his mouth stuffed. His look reveals that this would be a particularly bad time for him to have to saddle the horses. He looks expectantly at his boss and continues chewing carefully. The laird of the manor, who is very familiar to him, raises his eyebrow and gives him a smile. "Eat on, boy, I can do it alone for once. See to it that you get some meat on your bones and that your stomach calms down. Let Hailey pack up something for your old man. He'll definitely need it after his boozing last night. Wretched boozer!" He folds the letter carefully and puts it back in the envelope, and then gives Sam a decisive look. Sam quickly lowers his head as if he had been caught in a criminal act and hastily bites into a piece of bread. Hailey observes the strange behavior of the two and tries to draw conclusions from it. "You don't have to be ashamed of your father, do you understand, Sam? He is going through a difficult time and that has nothing to do with you! You are a good hardworking boy! Don't let anyone tell you anything else! Angus is already taking care of your father! Now eat on!" As soon as she utters these words, the two men exchange glances again and Angus stomps out of the kitchen.

With the reins held firmly in his hand, the usually calm Scotsman gallops excitedly from his yard towards civilization. The mane of his noble animal dances in the wind from the speed and his hooves send pebbles whirling up behind him. After a few kilometers, the astonished rider thinks about how fast the veterinarian must have gone on foot or that she left his guest house in the middle of the night. He has barely finished his thought when Aaron startles and shies at a figure coming out of the bushes on the side of the road. Angus expertly calms his stallion down and stops in the middle of the road. He extends his hand so the woman, now standing beside the horse. She then soothingly strokes the horse's strong neck.

"Breakfast is ready and if we're lucky, it will still be warm. Hailey doesn't like it when our guests leave the house hungry. You shouldn't start out on this long way to the mad village without some sustenance."

Chapter 41

"I beg your pardon?! To Switzerland?! No, this cannot be! You're pulling my leg!" Frank Conley, the former internationally known action film star, slowly sits down on the first available chair. The horror in his pale face makes him look older. He looks at Linda with big eyes and she covers his mouth with her hand, as if she wants to stop any further exclamations.

"I wish I were, Frank. Mirjam apparently has a schoolmate who likes to boast that his father works for the police and that he knows his passwords and access to their internal network... Apparently, his boasting wasn't just stupid chatter. And since he wanted to impress our daughter, he showed her the hack in an IT lesson. She logged in today and searched for Simon... and found this most recent entry."

She then also takes a seat at the dining table and supports her hands as if in prayer. She closes her eyes and continues, "You remember when Susan suddenly appeared in the psychiatric clinic and couldn't remember anything? The psychiatrist, Jeff Robinson, guessed back then, that she was experiencing the same drug effects like Roberto was. Only he was admitted involuntarily, but they didn't have enough time to get rid of Susie quickly." Frank nods thoughtfully and looks at Linda questioningly.

"Of course I remember that! How could I ever forget how strange Susie was acting? Like a trapped wild animal! But what are you trying to tell me?"

The former professor answers his question with concentration, saying, "I am telling you that we have been duped! We were cheated and lied to! Not only about Mirjam, but also about Simon!" Now she looks him straight in the eyes and the sparkle in her eyes does not bode well.

"But by whom? You don't think Susie...?!" His increased horror brings even more wrinkles to his forehead as he gives Linda an angry look.

"What about me?" Susan Manders appears in the open doorway like a genie who has been summoned from a bottle and smiles widely at the two serious faces at the table.

Chapter 42

At a leisurely pace, Aaron walks home on the gravel path with two passengers on his strong back. It seems as if he too is enjoying his owner's restored calm and the unusual company of a lady. Again and again, she strokes his neck and claps her hands in praise.

"You'd better not do that, otherwise he'll be spoiled!" Not sure if Angus is serious about this request or is joking in his dry way, Stacy pulls her hand back and grabs the saddle horn again. She feels his warm breath on the back of her neck and his big body close to hers. She is surprised that he is allowing such closeness, although he otherwise seems extremely distant and even shy. She notices that the longer she thinks about this and pays attention to how close his body is to hers, the more nervous she gets. She feels the blush creep into her face and her pulse starts to speed up. She desperately tries to distract her thoughts, clearing her throat, frowning and looking across the vastness of the Scottish Highlands.

"Would you rather I get down and walk next to you?" Surprised by his question, she looks over her shoulder in embarrassment.

"But no! What makes you think that?" She pushes her butt further forward and tries to look relaxed.

"That's exactly why!" Angus swings down from his horse and gives her the reins. "It's not far anymore anyway." He puts his hands in the pockets of his corduroy pants and walks with long steps at the level of the horse's head. Caught off guard and somewhat offended, the still nervous veterinarian watches the mysterious stranger from behind.

"Do you see the old, ramshackle house over there? Next to the stinking pigsty that you can smell all the way over here? Sam lives there." Angus points his hand in up towards the sky. Indeed, Stacy sees an old and neglected house.

"Oh... I'm sorry..." are the only words she says about it and cannot take her eyes off it.

"Hm... Yes, me too..." her companion replies and slides his hand through Aaron's mane. "The uninvited guest at the door last night was his father. He owns that palace over there." Without looking at it again, he nods his head in the direction he just pointed.

"How terrible... Poor boy..." the rider replies. A few seconds later, curiosity wins the fight against her decency and she asks, "What did he want from you?"

With a grin, Angus gives her one quick look and says, "Well, he just wants to pick a bone again with the damn rich son of the whore! He always wants that when he has emptied out his store of cheap schnapps and gets himself worked up with the village gossip." He slaps his stallion on the neck. Stacy can't figure out what he means by his answer and lets him know this, saying, "I don't follow what you're saying.

Why would you be a damn... well, you know what I mean?"

"Because my mother was the village whore! I told you – this has never been just about our family! And apparently my sister kept this detail secret from you in her stories."

Chapter 43

"That miserable, tiny, fat, slimy, piggish, greedy, venomous snake with a bald head!!!" Susan Manders' red face threatens to explode, and her plump breasts bounce up and down as she takes a deep breath. "I will have his clinic blown up and make sure he's tied to a bed inside of it! And then... And then I'll do the same with the oh-so-trustworthy American police! And... And... When I'm finished with THEM, then I'll wipe Simon's ugly ass with... With..."

Frank walks over to the ticking bomb of a woman and tries to calm her down. "Susie, calm down! That won't work now. We need a clear head to understand exactly what happened and who is behind it before we make any murderous plans." He gently puts a hand on her shoulder, but she won't allow this and rejects his kindness for the first time since their friendship started.

"No, my dear, enough is enough! I didn't like that bastard of a hospital manager from the moment I first set eyes on him! I thought he was revolting back then, but now I find out that this dog was one of the causes of all the misery this wonderful family has gone through! And what for?!" As she speaks, she goes over to Linda and stands demonstratively next to her.

"I cannot imagine what our sweet, brave Mirjam will have to go through now! The poor child! But she's as clever as a fox, right?!" Susie sits down on the chair next to Linda and observes the elegant Swiss woman. "Linda, how can you do it? Tell me your trick. How can you stay so calm?!"

Linda's brows droop a bit and her face hardens. "Unfortunately, it's not a secret recipe, Susan. I just lost a lot of my emotions... I wish I could show feelings the way you do so wonderfully... But I am rigid, wounded, scarred and chained inside." She puts her cold hand on top of Susan's warm, fleshy hand and adds, "But I agree with you. Enough is enough! You have never been to beautiful Switzerland, right?"

Chapter 44

"Oh my goodness! Miss Burns! That was by far the best breakfast I've ever had in my life! I'm about to explode! I think I can't even move anymore. Heavens! It all tastes wonderful!" As soon as she has finished giving free rein to her admiration, Stacy scoops up another spoonful of haggis and puts it on her plate.

"My dear, I'm very happy that you like it! And I am sure this will not be the last time you sit at our breakfast table, right, Angus? Wouldn't it be wonderful to have Stacy visit us often in the future?" She glances first at her guest, who continues chewing her food, and then looks curiously at the laird of the manor, who is chewing his food at the other end of the table while watching the veterinarian.

"I don't know... At this rate, I'm not sure we'll have any food left for future visits!" He points to Stacy with his fork, piled high with food, who is visibly ashamed and dabs at her mouth with the cloth napkin.

"Excuse me Angus ... But the trek this morning made me so hungry and..."

"Angus! You should be ashamed of yourself! Look at the way you're talking to Miss Stacy! Phooey! My good child, don't listen to this oaf! It is wonderful when a woman has an appetite and is not afraid to eat! All these skinny, starved girls that you see on TV today are terrible! Right, Angus? Men don't really like that, do they? We used to be required to have curves just to stand a chance. Only women who were well endowed and had feminine curves had good chances with men!" Hailey giggles and turns her head to Angus, who offers an innocent shrug. Stacy, on the other hand, shily glances downward as her attention moves towards her own curves.

"All right. Everything in the right place. And a veterinarian needs strength to do the job right." Angus inhales loudly through his nose and before he shoves the heaped fork into his mouth, he adds, "How did it happen that you chose this profession anyway? I remember that this was always Heather's dream... Is that a coincidence?" He puts the bite of bacon in his mouth and watches as emotions begin to dance on the veterinarian's face. Her secret, it appears, has been exposed.

Chapter 45

The mood in the limousine is a mixture of foul anger, bitter disappointment and hopeful confidence. Mirjam sits nestled close to Rosalía and occasionally wipes the tears rolling silently down her cheeks. Rosa gently strokes her dark, curly hair, which resembles her hair, and quietly suppresses the desire to break into a heated monologue with herself. Roberto looks out of the moving car and massages his thighs. He reaches for his cell phone, reads his wife's message again and bites his lower lip. He looks at his suffering daughter and wishes he could free her from pain. How much easier it is to lessen physical pain as a doctor than it is to heal a broken heart as a father.

"Papa, I just don't understand something..." Mirjam blows her nose as she sits upright and looks at her father sadly. He returns her gaze and fears all the questions to come, an emotion that Linda never had, which is why he has always envied her. 'Why have any fear if you don't know what will happen? Just wait, let things happen to you and then act in a focused manner...' How simple it sounds when she says it. He, on the other hand, has always feared the future and will continue to do so. Not because he likes this feeling – quite the contrary. Fear is uncomfortable and creeps through all his veins and tendons. No, it's because he learned to fear. As far back as he could recall, nothing was ever out of place; it was an easy childhood. Now, for the past few years, everything seems to have been going awry. How can he help his daughter, he wonders, when he hardly knows the answer himself? How difficult it is to be a parent. Anyone can be a parent, but can everyone be good at it?

"Are you listening to me at all?! Father? I asked you something?!" Mirjam's voice reveals is irritable and impatient, which he tries to appease with a tender smile. "Sorry, darling, my thoughts have just played a trick on me. No, I was not listening to you. Please repeat it. What is it that you don't understand?" He glances at Rosalia, who looks at him as if a baseball is about to hit him.

"I asked why this Simon guy wanted your child? It doesn't make sense to steal someone else's child! He had girlfriends himself?!" Desperate for more answers, Mirjam looks at her father, awaiting an answer. This exact question has been the source of Roberto's fears.

Chapter 46

Stacy dabs the corner of her mouth and leans back in her chair. "So now I definitely cannot take another bite! A thousand thanks, Miss Burns, for these wonderful treats!" She smiles at the white-haired lady and looks at Angus. "I know Heather would have been very happy if she knew I was having breakfast with you here. I have missed her every day since she has left us." Stacy carefully folds the cloth napkin on her lap and continues, "She not only raved about the two of you, but also about a woman named Bonnie. Who was she?" She looks up to find Angus looking at Hailey, as if in silent conversation. After a moment, Hailey smiles and Angus breaks the silence, "Well, since you have now eaten half my supply and Heather was your nanny, you are basically a member of the family, and you deserve to know the missing pieces of the puzzle of our family drama. After that, you can decide whether you want to stay or not."

Two surprised and astonished pairs of eyes stare at him.

"Angus! My boy! Is that true?! Can she stay?! Here with us at the manor?! Oh Angus! You make me so incredibly proud! I knew that deep inside you was a good, warm and..." A soft yet intrusive clearing of the throat interrupts Hailey's joyful outburst and she looks questioningly at Stacy, saying, "Is everything okay with you, my dear?! Isn't it wonderful?!" Stacy smiles, somewhat embarrassed.

"It is indeed a very generous offer, which I unfortunately have to reject. And this has nothing, but really nothing at all to do with your family history, which I would of course like to hear." She emphasizes this statement with a raised finger. "But, as much as I would like to stay here at this wonderful farm, with the wonderful animals and you both and Sam, I have a responsibility as a veterinarian in the village and..."

At this point she is interrupted by the laird, who says, "No one said that you are only allowed to come here and eat us out of house and home! Of course I don't want to see you here during the day! As far as I'm concerned, you can use the old cart in the garage to drive to work in the village. In the evening, a wonderful meal from our Hailey will await you, and if we feel like it, we can have a Viking drink together before you retire to the guest house." He knocks on the table with both fists and continues, "Besides, it can't hurt to have a veterinarian here at night. What do you think? Do you want to hear the story now or not?! Otherwise, I'm going out to the stable."

Chapter 47

"Mamá! Mamá!" Lively and loud, the twins hop down the steps of the Conley Villa in the

Hamptons and run across the pebbled driveway towards Rosalía. "Mis queridos! Hola cucarachas!! Have you missed mamá yet?! Qué pasa aquí?!" She kisses them both lovingly on the head and pinches them in the side. They both screech, racing away from her and then stop, standing frozen for a moment. "Pero, tío Roberto?! Dondé está tu silla de ruedas??!!"

"Uncle Roberto no longer needs his wheelchair! Your mom healed him!" With a smile, Roberto winks at the two rascals, who stand there with their mouths open in astonishment. He hugs his daughter sideways and walks with her towards the stairs. Linda comes through the open door, wearing an elegant, beige two-piece suit, and spreads her arms. Mirjam quickly breaks away from Roberto and runs up the stairs, directly into the open hug, which is for her only. "Mama!!!" She cries into her mother's white blouse, deeply inhaling this familiar flowery fragrance. Mirjam's delicate hands dig into mother's back as Linda's warm breath brushes against her hair. "We love you; you know that! And nothing will change at all! Do you understand me?!" Linda holds

119

her daughter tightly, emphasizing this statement with an extra squeeze. The sobs on her chest become softer and she hears a reassuring sniffing. "Mama, I... I want to find her... After all she's my... Well, you could say she's my sister, right? I've always wanted a sister..."

"I'm ready to go!" Susie races frantically through the door and looks at the faces in front of her. "Hey! You're already here! Great, then let's go! I don't want to go home in the flying rattletrap. I'm a lady with the big butt on the floor... Well, with an elegant leather seat in between... Still, you understand what I mean!" She walks up to Mirjam, frees her from the first embrace and pulls her in for a new one.

"My girl!!! My big brave girl!!! Susie and your mom will now grab this bull by the horns and..." She sees Linda's slightly reproachful look and hesitates in the middle of her sentence, then continues, "Oh crap! My big mouth opened too quickly once again... Excuse me... I'm sorry... I have no idea when I will finally learn..."

Confused, Mirjam looks from Susie to her mother and then to Roberto, who has walked over to them in the meantime and is now holding Linda by the waist.

"Mama? Papa? What's going on here? What does she mean by that?"

Chapter 48

Her eyes filled with tears, Stacy looks first at the storyteller and then at the lady of the manor. She wipes the tears from her eyes with her sleeves, like a child, and swallows audibly. "So, in other words, Heather's misfortune was my best childhood memory?! That's horrible! Angus! Miss Burns?!" Now she casts horrified looks from one pair of eyes to the other.

"Well, if that's how you want to look at it, Doctor." Angus simultaneously raises his shoulders and eyebrows, and Hailey immediately hisses at him, "How can you say that! Angus! You should be ashamed of yourself!" Then she turns to Stacy and says, in a calm and sad tone, "No, my dear! Not at all!

Your family was exactly the joy our beloved Heather needed. You made her so happy! And I will soon be able to prove that to you as soon as..." She gets up and approaches Angus. She steps behind him and puts her hand on his shoulder as if to calm him down before the end of her sentence, continuing "...as soon as my sister is here."

Stacy has to wipe away the tears rolling softly down her cheeks again before she finds her voice, and says, "Bonnie? She's coming here?! Oh, how nice for you, Miss Burns! You must be really excited, right?! When is she coming?" As soon as she has finished, she notices Angus' serious face next to Hailey's hand. "Oh... She isn't coming alone... Am I right?"

"No, my dear, she isn't coming alone. She is bringing her part of our family. And for this reason, you will stay with us in the main house and not in the guest house." As she says this, her hand pats Angus' shoulder.

The guest sitting at the table seems to understand what the generous host was planning.

She pushes her chair away from the table and stands up. She carefully places her napkin on the table and looks at the astonished lady of the house, saying "With all my heart, I would like to thank you once again for this great breakfast, Miss Burns! I wish you a happy reunion with Bonnie and her family and who knows, maybe I can get to know her. I would very much like to tell you how much your niece, wife and mother meant to me and what incredible influence she still has on my life!"

Chapter 49

Deep in thought, Frank paces back and forth in front of the large window with a breathtaking view of the sea. He mumbles incomprehensible words to himself and stops walking periodically.

"I don't know, boys, I don't know..." He addresses the two men who are in the room with him. Roberto sips from his water glass and looks out of the window. Kenneth steps over next to his father and addresses them both, saying "What is there to lose? Two flights, right? You can keep the jetlag at no charge." He smiles at his father and turns to Roberto. "I think this is important for Linda, after all these years. Of course, Claudia could pursue this in Switzerland, right? But I haven't seen your wife look so determined in ages... As if her old fighting spirit had come back to life! I remember it like it was yesterday when she ran down the hall after reading Simon's message that you were alive and staying at the clinic! You remember, right Dad?" He looks over at his father.

"No!" Frank crosses his arms over his chest and stands with his legs apart in front of the window. "She stays!" These words come very clearly out of his mouth. Ken and Roberto look at each other questioningly and Conley Junior attempts to dispel the confusion, saying, "What do you mean, Dad?"

"I said no! She is not traveling to Switzerland!" Frank Conley doesn't move a millimeter, standing motionless in his statue position.

Now Roberto stands up, straightens his leather belt on his jeans and takes slow steps towards Frank. Carefully, as if he did not want to chase away a shy animal, he speaks to him from the side. "Frank, what do you know?" The big Swiss man stands next to the former action hero and looks at him seriously.

"You know something? Tell us."

***

"Mama, when did you find out about Simon?" Mirjam sits cross-legged on the big box spring bed and watches her mother packing.

"What did I find out, darling?" Linda carefully places the folded trousers in the open suitcase, which is also on the bed. She concentrates on the jewelry on the dressing table and asks again when she does not receive an answer, "When did I find out WHAT, Mirjam?!" A little excited, she turns and looks at the sad and confused face of the teenage girl. Silent tears roll down her flushed cheeks and Linda understands.

"Hmm... I see... Papa told you about that also..." Linda sits down next to her daughter and hugs her fiercely.

"I wanted to know why he wanted your baby so much... It's sick!... Even if he was in love with Papa... Who does that? Do you think he wanted to kill Papa when he found everything out?!"

Linda releases her daughter from the hug and tries to comfort Mirjam, saying, "No, my sweetheart, I'm sure he didn't want to kill Papa. It was a terrible accident that he also wanted to cover up... He was the one who brought Papa to this clinic to be helped. And he wanted to be close to him, that's why he started an internship there." As she listens to herself, she notices how she is defending Simon to appease her daughter. This fact ignites her anger once again and she presses her lips tightly together.

Chapter 50

"Bye Sam! It was nice to see you again! Watch out for Miss Burns!" As he walks past, Stacy waves to the stable boy, who she is now looking at with different eyes. He waves to her cautiously and continues walking towards the pile of horse manure with his head bowed and the pitchfork in his hand.

She takes a final look at the dreamlike house of the McKay family and waves to Hailey Burns, who is standing at the window, watching her wistfully. What a terrible family tragedy they all had to witness. Stacy mentally reviews the stories told by Angus as she strolls through the pristine Scottish landscape.

Angus' father must have been an extremely generous and good-natured man. He took in the three sisters, married the pregnant woman in order to adopt the unborn child as a father, although Heather was not his biological daughter. When her mother died at birth, the two aunts raised her at the manor. Unfortunately, Stacy was never allowed to find out how strong family love can be. Her father was happy when housekeepers, nannies and doctors took care of her so that he could be at his bank every minute. Manage money, make even more money, steal money from others... The main thing is money, money and more money! What a blessing that Heather came to them and that Stacy was finally able to feel love, care and security.

And then the village whore... It all sounds like something out of a Hollywood movie. He fell in love with the village whore... The sister of Sam's father...who was also her suitor... What a bastard... One terrible fate, after another. But why Angus' mother no longer wanted to go to the manor and got away with it is still a mystery... Was it possible Heather's brother also... It's better if she doesn't know that either...

The veterinarian shakes her head, rubs her arms and hugs herself. Yes, she can understand Angus. She can understand very well why he does not like this Frank Conley... This superhero stole the most important person away from both of them. Simply took her away with him and carried her far away!

Chapter 51

Frank looks at the two men seriously and puts his hands on his hips. He takes a deep breath and wipes his face with one hand. "I called Mayer. He was the only normal member of this gang..." As the concerned grandfather speaks, he goes to the bar and takes a full bottle from the shelf. He pours the whisky into three glasses and his two listeners accept this gesture as an invitation. Both walk over to stand next to him and take a glass.

"I told him about Mirjam's discovery and tried to be as factual as possible. Without much success obviously." He takes a large swallow from his glass, emptying it. He pours himself more whisky and walks over to the window, glass in hand." I didn't like that slimy shit Tropman right from the start! Just like in my films... all money-hungry, lying police officers. Who can you trust today?!"

"Frank, please, could you get to the point?!" Roberto sips from his glass nervously and follows the actor over to the window. Ken does the same and crosses his arms over his chest.

"He looked at the internal investigation and found no further entries... Therefore, no further activities were undertaken... Actually, Simon never left Mexico! The entry about Switzerland was misleading to provide a distraction from the actual facts. And because Simon is Swiss, it would of course have made sense that he was looking for shelter in his home country since no one was looking for him there and we could not have proven anything." Two pairs of eyes look at him in surprise.

"Wait, what?! But that can't be... Mike said he..." And before Roberto can finish his sentence, Frank takes over for him, saying "...had to drop him off at the clinic landing site because he had to do something first before flying to Costa Rica, right!? Then they all went to the clinic to find Dr. Robinson, the American psychiatrist, do you remember?" Roberto feels icy cold sweat soak his skin and he also empties his glass in one swallow.

"Yes, exactly, he 'treated' Susie and Mike." He makes quotation marks in the air with his fingers as he says this and adds, "And after that, the film fades to black." Frank claps his hands.

"But Dad, how do you know that Simon didn't leave Mexico?! And what does Tropman have to do with it? Why would someone put a misleading entry about Switzerland in a police file? I don't understand...?!" Visibly irritated, Kenneth shakes his head.

"Tropman was in on the whole thing with them from the very beginning. That slimy shit participated in all of it! You may remember who supported the fat little bald guy?" He scrutinizes his son carefully and nods, continuing, "Yes, exactly, the police... But not the Mexican police, as we thought, no, it was our...our police! Not the FBI, no, the Coney Island Police Department! Can you even believe it? Do you understand what's going on?!" Frank takes a step towards his bar, opens the bottle of single malt and pours generously into the glass.

Roberto takes big steps towards Frank, clanks his glass down on the bar and looks at the actor reproachfully saying, "You don't actually expect us to take you seriously when you say that that madhouse is holding innocent American citizens against their will?!! Frank!?" He slams his hand down onto the wooden top of the bar. Frank looks at him, and then at both men, with a disappointed look on his face.

"Unfortunately, that's not all...!"

Chapter 52

Angus gently strokes his mare's neck, along her elegant back and over her strong flank. He walks close to her so that she can feel his body heat. He steps around her and does the same on the other side. She enjoys his closeness, but steps nervously from hoof to hoof, snorting loudly.

"You will do great, my beauty! Together we will do great. Nothing more than what we trained on; I promise you. There will be more people watching and admiring you, but I will be there, and Sam will be there and we three will show everyone what you can do. OK? Let's do this?! The three of us, together? Good girl!" Angus deliberately stands close to her neck and feels her pressure against him. He smiles and knows that she understands him better than any human female could. He takes the comb out of the box and gently begins combing her mane, braiding it and tying ribbons at the ends of the braids. His soothing, loving words reach the pricked ears of the white horse.

"I can do that, cousin Angus." The stable boy stands in the open door and holds out his hands. Without looking up, the owner of the manor ties a final bow at the end of a braid of thick horse hair and grunts deeply, saying, "You're not supposed to eavesdrop on people... Did your drunk old man never teach you that?" He continues combing the horse's mane calmly and makes a gesture at the boy with his head. "We are not family, so don't call me that! Nothing has changed. I'm the boss here and you are the stable boy, do you understand? Now take a comb so you can finally learn how to make a lady pretty!"

A tender, loving smile flits across Hailey's face as she watches them. She takes a deep breath and closes her eyes for a split second. She takes the cross on her necklace into her hand and glances quickly at the cloudy sky above her. "This is working out well, isn't it? This is all working out really well!" Softly she whispers these words as a tear rolls down her wrinkled cheek. "He's a good boy, my Angus... Such a good boy..." She turns around and starts to walk towards the house when she sees a car driving into the courtyard. She frowns in amazement and takes a step forward before stopping in shock.

"Officer Hunter? What brings you here to visit us? I hope a courtesy call before the big day?"

Chapter 53

Distraught and silent, all three men sit on the leather furniture and look at each other. "What should we do next? This will hit Rosalía like a tornado... It will break her heart if she finds out what was really going on with her patients and colleagues... I wonder if Pablo really died of blood poisoning back then..." Ken rubs his face with both hands as if trying to clear it of dust. He throws himself backwards against the backrest of his seat and combs through his thick hair with his hand. "Oh Holy Justice! There is SO MUCH to do now!!! How is all of this even possible?! i just can't... No, I just don't want to believe... Oh God!!" He suddenly sits up straight and looks at the equally dismayed Roberto. "Carmelita and her family! The nursery school children! Rosalía was just... But what... Who... I... I need to get some fresh air! I can't breathe in here!... I..."

Just then, Bonnie steps into the room and looks at Kenneth, startled. She says, "My boy! What is wrong with you?! Are you not feeling well?! You are white as a sheet! Frank?! What's going on here?!" She tries to take hold of Conley Junior's arm, but he hurries past her as if he's being chased. She puts both hands over her mouth and turns to Conley Senior.

"He'll calm down soon. You know him. As soon as his factual legal brain is involved, he will be standing firmly again. I just delivered some bad news and this time it also involves his family... He can't look at the facts quite yet. Loving another person is not only beautiful..." With these words, he looks at Roberto and bends forward. "Should we all go on the trip? What do you think?"

Bonnie takes a step towards Frank and before Roberto can answer, she asks, "Switzerland is a false alarm, am I right?" After Frank's silent nod, she continues, "There is never a good time for bad news, Frank..." She stops in front of him and waits for him to make eye contact. Roberto asks, "Bonnie, what happened? The girls?!" The small Scottish woman shakes her head and looks at Roberto with tear-filled eyes. Frank, too, now realizes that this is no longer about his message and gets up. He takes his housekeeper, friend and the aunt of his late wife by the shoulders and looks at her meaningfully.

"They came and took our boy. He is suspected...of murder!"

Chapter 54

Angus looks calmly and emotionlessly into the pair of eyes opposite him and clicks his tongue, saying, "That's it! There was nothing more! Even if you ask me the same question a hundred times. Can I go now? I have a lady waiting for me." He starts to rise from his chair when a wave of a hand stops him. The policeman opposite him shakes his head hopelessly and angrily.

"Damn it, MacKay! Can't you understand that this situation is serious?!" Angrily, he takes the folded file from the table in front of him, opens it and slams it down on the table in front of Angus.

"Look at what you are accused of! Yes, look closely and then I want to know if anyone can testify that you have nothing to do with it?!" He points menacingly at the photo between them, then at Angus' motionless face.

"I don't kill people. I don't like them, certainly, but I don't take their lives. And this dog here..." He takes a quick look at the picture and continues, "I don't... Sorry, I DIDN'T LIKE him very much at all... But I don't throw drunk old men into the gorge! And you know that, Officer Hunter! So just stay away from me with your lying allegations and let me do my work in the yard, understand!?" The strong Scotsman once again rises from his folding chair and starts to leave the room when he is verbally restrained.

"Who told you he was drunk? Listen... We have a statement against you, Angus. You're being charged. I can't just let you go like that." James

Hunter gets up and walks towards the big Scotsman, who is standing at the door. He starts to put his hand on Angus' shoulder but stops and puts both of his hands on his hips.

"Could someone testify, that you didn't touch a hair on his head?! It's important, Angus, damn it, something is happening here! And obviously you know more than you want to admit. Without a counter-statement, I can't..."

"What about Hailey? You don't believe her, either?" With hatred in his eyes, Angus looks first at the ceiling, then at the policeman.

The policeman shakes his head and tilts it down to look at the floor. "No, that's not possible! She is like your birth mother. She would do anything for you, everyone knows that!"

Angus turns slowly and looks around the barren room. He crosses his arms and nods, saying, "Ahh, yes, I understand... Everyone knows so much here, don't they? Everyone knows that I... We ...live alone at the big manor house... The strange old lady and the screwed-up son of a whore... Everyone

138

knows that the bastard child fled to Hollywood and everyone knows that we are swimming in money and exploiting poor Sam, even though my mother was his aunt... And the drunken dog has no money and I don't help him, although somehow he belongs to our clan... Yeah, I understand exactly what everyone here knows... The hinterland Highlander, who does it with his own horses because no person will do it with him... Sure... He also kills an annoying, drunk, innocent father! Yes, everyone here knows, right??!!"

Chapter 55

"What's a joint session, mamá?" One of the twins tries to climb onto his mother's lap while she tries to comb his wild curls.

"What do you mean by that? Who said anything about a joint session, mi amor?!" The beautiful Mexican woman throws her comb on the elegant dressing table in annoyance and helps her son climb up onto his mother's lap. She gently traces his light eyebrows with her index finger and runs it over his small pouty mouth.

139

"How could such a light-skinned little person have come out of me? Your Scottish veins still have priority... Well, I would have sworn that the dark predominates! So, you said 'joint session'? Where did you hear that, Cucaracha?"

"Baba said that to Papa and looked at him very angry!" The large, round, light green eyes look at Rosalía with interest and concern at the same time. She frowns and bites her full lower lip.

"Ha... Interesting... He said a joint session? Are you sure about that?" She pulls on one of his curls and looks at his twin brother, who is sitting next to them on the bed and fiddling with a toy excavator. "Did you hear that too, AJ?" She gives the bed a light kick with her foot to get her son's attention. He shakes his head without looking up and replies, "No, I heard that Baba needs a nasty session. For everyone!" He points a finger demonstratively in the air as if imitating his grandfather.

A mischievous smile flits across the mother's face as she concentrates and her white teeth flash. "Ahh, a nasty session! Gosh, what is Baba planning for us?!" She looks mysteriously from one pair of excited eyes to the other and smiles lovingly at her two boys. "You don't have to worry, mis cucarachas! Baba was definitely talking about a family crisis session! And that's nothing mean or nasty, it's just a name for a long conversation, where everyone can share their ideas and thoughts when a very important topic concerns the family." Both twins are now looking at their mother with even more interest than before and AJ asks, "Like the story that Daddy always tells where they all have to sit by the fire with their swords and dresses and hide?" Rosalía laughs loudly and throws her head back.

"Yes, just like the Scots when they had to prepare for the fight against the English. But these are not dresses, mi querido, they are kilts. Skirts for men. Like those that Papa and Baba have. And we certainly won't have to go off to a fight... At least I hope not..." She takes the grinning boy from her lap and gently throws him on the bed next to his brother. "And soon, yes very soon, you two will also be in two dresses like those, wrapped up like little fajitas! And you will look stunning in them!" She throws herself happily on the bed with them and tickles her two bundles of joy.

Chapter 56

"Angus, listen to me now!" The equally upset village policeman tries to soothe his former schoolmate. He starts to put his hand on his shoulder when the door opens. A small, stocky woman wearing a thick wool sweater and a checkered skirt stands in the open doorway. She is wearing glasses and is staring sternly at the paper in her hand.

"Angus MacKay, we received a call to stop interrogation immediately. You are still under suspicion, but you can leave the police station. You must not leave the MacKay property until you are called in for the next checks. Your only contact person outside your property will be your lawyer, who will also inform you of the next steps. You must hand over your mobile phone right now to Officer Hunter and sign here. Do you have any questions, Mr. MacKay?" The small Scotswoman takes off her glasses and looks closely at Angus.

"Who called?! Who was that?!" Hunter intervenes without being asked. The female messenger gives him a disapproving glance and replies, "I didn't know that your last name was also MacKay?!" With no emotion, she turns her head back to Angus and waits for his reaction. He raises both hands in the air and murmurs, "I'm leaving! No cell phone, so no autograph session!" He pushes past the woman in the sweater and takes a final look over his shoulders.

James Hunter hastily grabs the piece of paper in the woman's wrinkled hands and reads through what's written on it. "Bloody hell! Of course, Hollywood has to get involved!" Angrily, he whirls the paper up in the air and looks at his still calm colleague. He notices the grin on her lips and crosses his arms. "What did he promise you?! Tell me! An autograph on your wool undershirt? Shit, Betty, this is serious here! We have a dead man! This is not a cow that was run over. This is a HUMAN!!!" He throws his hands up in the air and puts them on his head.

"Glasgow will tear me apart! I'll be the perfect fodder for them down there! I can already hear them with their Highlander jokes!"

143

Chapter 57

Frank Conley paces up and down in his classically furnished study, with a concentrated and stern look on his face. Linda sits on a chair with her hands clasped, directly in front of the large desk, and lets her gaze move around the room. She realizes that in all the years she has known Frank, she has never been in here. Why does an actor need a study with a desk anyway? Linda makes a mental note to ask Frank when all of this is over. Still unsure of why everyone is supposed to gather here, she gives Rosalía a questioning look. Sitting next to her, Rosalía glances around the room, seemingly with the same thought process as Linda.

Linda clears her throat and is about to open her mouth when Susie, who has just arrived, interrupts her.

"Hell and damnation, Conley Senior! If you have something to say to me, you'll have to sit your muscular butt in the hot tub! You already know how much work it is to get a luxurious body like mine out of the water again?! I just got in! If the flight is already postponed, then I want to be at least butter-soft for it! Where's the fire?! Oh... greetings, my darlings! Did he order you here, too?!" Surprised, she looks first at Linda's face, then at Rosalia's, and puts both hands on her cheeks." You are both so beautiful! If I could, I would paint you on the spot!" She gives them an admiring smile, then immediately turns to Frank, putting both hands on her full hips. "So, who ate what? What is going on here, honey bunch?!"

The former action hero looks at the door through which his son Kenneth enters with his mobile phone at the ear. "Thank you very much, Betty! I... We appreciate this very much! And of course you will be able to inform Frank Conley personally of this shortly. I'll make sure of that, as sure as the fact that my last name is Conley! Goodbye, Betty. Yes... That is correct... Exactly... You are absolutely right, Miss Betty... Oh, I beg your pardon, Miss Betty... Of course... Goodbye, Betty!" He quickly removes the phone from his ear and presses the off key. He closes his eyes for a moment. When he opens them again, he notices that everyone in the room is looking at him in surprise.

145

"So, Miss Betty...??!!" is the first sarcastic remark he hears from his petite wife. She raises an eyebrow and casually crosses one leg over the other without looking away from him.

"Nana, sweetie, that sounded like something from a previous semester! Rather my age class, you know? Besides that, she was obviously keen on my Franky! So, out with it, Ken, who is this Betty person?!" Susie demonstratively stands in front of the jeans-wearing professor and winks at him. Exhausted, he drops onto the chair right next to him and rubs his eyes. He then replies, "Betty is the district secretary of..." Before he finishes his sentence, they hear Roberto's slow, shuffling steps approach. When he steps through the door a few seconds later, he puts his hand on the door frame and takes a deep breath.

"The twins are watching a movie, Mirjam is with them and Bonnie will come here as soon as she gives the kiddos some snacks to munch on. So we can get started, Frank."

Chapter 58

Hailey excitedly paces in front of the magnificent stone house in the north of the Scottish Highlands. She holds her hands folded in front of her face and murmurs soft prayers. From afar, she hears an engine noise and looks up nervously. A rusty police car slowly drives along the gravel driveway and stops right in front of Hailey. She wipes her sweaty hands on her lace apron and waits expectantly for the passenger door to open. Instead of this, one of the rear doors opens and Angus' head slowly emerges.

"Oh, my boy! Thank God you are well and back home! She quickly walks over and holds him by the hand as she gazes up lovingly. After making sure that nothing is wrong, she bends down slightly and throws a derogatory look at the driver.

"You should be ashamed of yourselves! Shame on you! What would your grandmother say if she knew what bad things you are doing to decent people here, James Hunter!?" She raises her index finger menacingly as Angus gently pulls her away from the car.

"That's not Hunter." He nods to the driver and slams the car door. Knowing how stressful and disturbing these hours have been for his loyal companion, he gently puts his arm around her shoulders and accompanies her into the house.

"What delicious food is there for lunch?" He opens the big door like a gentleman and gestures with his arm for here to enter. "M'lady, after you!" As a thank you, he receives a slap from her kitchen towel and an angry look.

"How can you think about food now, Angus Cunningham MacKay?! You sit down right this minute and tell me what happened there?! I'm dying of worry and you want to eat!" Theatrically, she throws a hand over her head and puts it on her hip.

"But I don't want to sit on the cold floor here. Let's go to the kitchen. Then we can both get something out of it." With a mischievous grin, he walks past the small woman and follows the wonderful smell of roasted meat. He knew she would be waiting for him with a big delicious meal. When he steps into the kitchen, he stops for a moment, a look of surprise and a frown on his face. Walking past the guest at the table, he opens the refrigerator and takes an ale out.

"Angus! It's just past noon and you want to start drinking beer already? Tomorrow is the jumping competition! You have to prepare with a clear head!" He glances at Hailey with an even more irritated look on his face and shakes his head barely noticeably. "What do you mean? Since when is there a time of day for drinking an ale?!" He walks around the table, noisily places his beer on the wooden table, leans on the chair in front of him with both hands and looks emotionlessly into the pair of eyes opposite him.

"I can't ride tomorrow! But I assume word has already got around, and that is why YOU are sitting in my kitchen?!"

Chapter 59

Rosalía's sobs on Ken's shoulder, Susie's narrowed eyes, Linda's thoughtful pacing back and forth in the room, and Frank's nervous finger drumming on the table let Bonnie know that the important information has already been communicated. She walks quietly over to Roberto, who has buried his face in his hands, and touches him gently on the shoulder. As if awoken from sleep, he looks up at her with a start and takes a deep breath. He presses his lips together and speaks, "Bonnie is here now..." All eyes are focused on the small Scotswoman, who slowly folds her hands and looks from one pair of eyes to the next. She stops at Frank and looks at him questioningly. When there is no verbal reaction from him, she says, "I understand... Well, who is going to Scotland with me and who is going to Mexico?"

Everyone in the room looks at each other in confusion. Rosalía jumps up, swallows her last tears and touches her head, saying, "Caramba! Qué estúpida! Of course! We'll split up! Thanks, Bonnie!" She sends air kisses to her with both hands and then looks at her astonished husband. Frank stops drumming his fingers, leaving them on the table top, and nods silently. Roberto rises uncertainly and grabs Bonnie by the shoulders. "As usual, our Bonnie is calm, focused on the fact, well organized and prepared! I think that's a very good idea! The only question that remains is what the best possible distribution would be."

A loud snort is heard, and all eyes wander over to Susie. She shakes her head and looks angrily at the floor. "Well, I don't usually impose... But I have to finish something with the Nachos! Something very personal, if you understand?" At that moment, as soon as she has finished speaking, she realizes how thoughtless this statement is and looks at Linda apologetically, saying, "Sorry, honey, how stupid of me! Of course you understand and that was presumptuous of me... But... I'm boiling with anger!!! I definitely want to go to Mexico! Please! I... I... WE have to end this now!" She quickly draws an imaginary circle in the air.

"I want to go to Scotland! Please, mi amor! Let's go to Scotland! You have to go there either way, you are needed, and I am fed up with Mexico! I can't go there after finding out everything I now know! Por favor!!" The former physiotherapist gets on her knees and literally begs her husband. He lovingly pulls her up and hugs her. "I would never have allowed you to set one foot back in that clinic!" And with a questioning look at his father, he asks, "Dad?"

Chapter 60

"Why not?! I can do it!! Honestly! And we would still have time today to go through the important details so that it will work exactly as you imagine! What can we lose if we don't try?!" Excited and full of motivation and vigor, Stacy babbles at the stubborn Scots in front of her. She glances at Hailey, who is sitting quietly at the table, tracing the wooden leaves of table with her fingers.

Angus takes a deep breath, pulls his hand out of his corduroy pants pocket and waves his finger back and forth in front of the nervous veterinarian. "That is why it won't happen!" He raises an eyebrow and pulls his hand back again. He bends his upper body down to her so that her eyes are level with his and gives her a smile that confuses her and makes her even more nervous. After a few seconds, which seem like long, uncomfortable minutes, he opens his

152

mouth slowly and whispers, "You are much too nervous, M'lady! With you on my mare, I will lose EVERYTHING!" He winks at her and rises to his full height again.

"But, Angus! She means well and wants to help! Once again!" Hailey looks at both of them now and rises from her chair, continuing, "Have you ever thanked her for calling Ken for you?! You ungrateful Scot!? And how can you two actually think about the jumping event tomorrow?!" She turns energetically around in a circle and wipes the tears from her eyes with the kitchen towel, addressing Stacy. "Excuse me, dear, that I'm talking to you like this, but..." The small lady of the manor turns back to the two surprised faces and adds, dismayed, "Sam has lost his father in a terrible way! He is part of our family. You and Angus are under suspicion of taking a life!!! What kind of role does this event tomorrow play in this whole mess?!"

Stacy looks at the floor, ashamed, and purses her lips in embarrassment, saying, "You're right, Miss Hailey, I'm very sorry... I... I just know how important tomorrow is for..." Slowly, she looks up at Angus, who is still looking at Hailey. He then looks at the veterinarian and squeezes his eyes shut. He wrinkles his forehead, then clicks his tongue before saying, "I didn't know that you... Who called... I just wanted to get out... Thank you very much!" He then nods his head and directs his words and gaze to Hailey, "As is so often the case, you are right! Sam is part of our family... And that's exactly what we'll show everyone tomorrow!"

Chapter 61

"I would also like to go to Mexico..." A gentle voice penetrates the room full of emotions. Roberto turns around in surprise and looks into his daughter's sad eyes. Linda walks quickly over to her and takes her into her arms with care.

"But of course you'll come with us! We are family!" She kisses Mirjam on her curly hair and feels Roberto join in the hug.

Susan Manders rises from the armchair and smoothes her floral dress. "I don't think I need as many layers in the boiling hell as I packed for the mountains. Bonnie, can I leave some clothes here?" She looks at the nodding Scotswoman and turns to Frank. "And you! Whatever you choose, you are and will always be my superhero! Understood?! And I think I speak for everyone present here! We love you and are grateful for everything you have done and will do for each of us, old fellow! Follow your heart as always and we will meet you again at the end of your path! But decide for YOURSELF!" She winks at him and blows air kisses him from a distance.

Frank Conley rises from his barely used leather armchair behind the large desk and looks first into his son's face. Ken is holding his small wife by the shoulders and looks at his father with concern. He knows what a difficult decision he is facing. Frank's gaze wanders over to Bonnie, who also gives him an understanding look, and then he smiles at Susie. Six tired pairs of eyes watch for an answer. They all are family by way of Linda, who has been like his own flesh and blood for years, look at him sadly and tiredly.

The former action hero lowers his gaze as he becomes enveloped in thoughts and images. Friends, family and the duty to do right, seem to collide so often in this life, and here he is again. As Frank sinks down into the armchair, he pauses for a moment, allowing the silence to settle.

"I once had an exceptional role in a movie. A movie that did not fit in with the rest of my portfolio and yet I loved playing that role..."

Everyone looks at him with surprise and curiosity as he continues, "And in this role, there was one line that I would never have thought would be quotable until now..."

Chapter 62

Excitedly taking small hasty steps, Hailey walks across the large gravel yard to the stables. "Sam?! Sam, boy, where are you?! Sam?!!" She has not yet reached the stable gate, so she calls out as loudly as her vocal cords will allow her to. But there is no trace of the calm lad. The small Scotswoman shakes her head. She can't even imagine how he is feeling. She hasn't seen him since the bad news. But he must be here. Where else could he be? Except for his father, he had no one and he has long been old enough to live on his own. At the next opportunity and when the worst part of this is over, she may even ask him why he didn't leave his father. That must have been a hellish living situation for Sam, living with that scoundrel. With this thought, she hastily crosses herself and whispers, "This is not the way to talk about the dead!"

She enters the stables and starts to call the name of their family member again. No answer still. She goes from horse stall to horse stall and carefully looks inside each one, calling, "Sam? Are you here, my boy? Please come, the food is on the table! Stacy is here, too... And Angus is back too... He's waiting for you... He needs to tell you something urgently... Sam?" She gets to the last horse stall, which is empty, and crosses her arms in disappointment. She is about to go back to the gate when she hears a sound from the open loft area. She looks up into the darkness and squints her eyes, calling out, "Sam, my boy, are you up there? You know I can't climb this ladder, so please, my good boy, come down!" She once again hears a pawing sound and wrinkles her forehead. "Sam! Please don't play hide-and-seek now and come with me! We are here for you! You belong to our family! Come on now, you must be starving!" She hears a bottle clink and dragging footsteps. A little hay falls down in front of her feet and she sees Sam's red hair emerging from the shadows.

"For God's sake, Sam!!! My boy, are you drunk??!!" She puts both hands over her mouth and hardly dares to breathe. She looks at the swaying boy up in the high loft and holds one hand in the air as if to stop him. "Stand there Sam! Or better yet, sit or lie down slowly. I'll get Angus! Stay where you are, for heaven's sake, Sam!? My boy! I'll go get Angus! Stay there! No, sit down! Sam! Poor Sam! Oh God!!"

As she quickly leaves the stable, she repeatedly crosses herself and sends hurried prayers up to heaven. No sooner have her feet stepped onto the gravel than she screams for Angus at the top of her lungs, so loudly that the horses behind her start whinnying just as loudly.

158

Chapter 63

Frank Conley looks mysteriously at the circle of tense faces, enjoying the silent attention for a moment.

"I'll take over the headquarters and hold the position!" As soon as he has finished saying this, Roberto points his finger at the action hero and quickly says, as if he were in a quiz show, "Stolen Lives! A thriller, published in 2020!" As if he has just won a million dollars, he looks at the amazed group of people with a huge smile on his face and slaps his hand on his leg, which makes him start swaying. Conley Senior winks happily at him and replies, "Good boy!"

Susie rolls her eyes, throws both hands over her head and leaves the room, shaking her head. "Headquarters! Thriller! I'll start a thriller myself with these... These...!"

Bonnie starts to follow her in silence, with her head bowed, when Frank stops her by saying, "Bonnie! You understand me, right? As soon as all this mess is over, I'll follow! I promise! OK? Bonnie?"

He waits, full of hope, for her reaction, which, to his disappointment, does not turn out as he hoped. She looks back sadly and says quietly, "Fear is not a threat, Frank! But I am trying to understand." She turns around again and leaves the room.

"It's OK, Dad. She has been looking forward to all of us going there for so long. The story with Angus now gets the two sisters out of their little houses. But we are with her and we will make things right! Don't worry, your initial disappointment will be over soon." Ken walks over to his father, who is still sitting, not moving, behind the desk, looking at the open door.

"No, it's not OK, my son! She is right, I'm afraid! Extremely afraid, actually! I can't even imagine what has accumulated over all these years inside of him... I have simply been too cowardly to show up since the accident!"

"That's not true, Frank!" Linda intervenes now, continuing, "You wanted to go there... And throw tree trunks with me... Do you remember?" She looks at him lovingly and gratefully. "But then we went to

Mexico and acquired a big family! That was anything but cowardly of you! And we will all be forever grateful to you to the ends of our lives for your selfless heroic deeds!"

"And it is exactly these stories that we will spread in Scotland! I'm small, but I have the temper of four people put together! And since I can no longer talk to myself, my need for communication is never fulfilled anyway! So caramba, I want to tell this mysterious, muscular, two-meter tall, red-haired, wild Highlander in his kilt what is really going on here!" Rosalía claps her hands loudly and violently to give her statement even more determination.

Her husband raises an eyebrow questioningly, puts both hands on his hips and grins, saying, "That's how you imagine Angus?"

Chapter 64

"Jump, I said! Damn it, let yourself fall, you drunk pile of shit!" Angus roars angrily up to the loft and looks sternly at the swaying stable boy. Hailey

161

holds one hand on her mouth anxiously, and with the other, she clings to Stacy's arm next to her. "For heaven's sake, the poor boy will break all his bones!" Following this statement, the land owner shakes his head and does not take his eyes off Sam.

"No, he won't! Not if he falls on the straw! But I will break all his bones MYSELF as soon as he's down here! Do you understand me, you idiot!?! And now get your skinny ass down here and let me knock some sense into you!"

"Well, I'm not a psychologist... But I don't think it will work that way..." Stacy's looks sympathetically from Angus up to Sam and she speaks to him in a soft voice, saying, "It's okay, Sam. Nothing will happen to you. I'll make sure of it!" She glances at Angus, who rolls his eyes at the same time. "I can understand very well what you're going through, Sam! Really! This is terrible and hurts incredibly badly! And no one can take that pain away, you see? Not even the alcohol, Sam! Especially not that! It makes everything much worse. Take a close look at Angus!" He looks at Stacy in amazement and waits to see what comes next. The veterinarian, who remains calm, does not get upset and looks at Sam closely, saying, "He is angry about the alcohol, not with you, Sam! He is angry about how drinking changes you! Because he is incredibly proud and has very high expectations of you! You will see, Sam! But now you have to jump down to us! Here on the straw! I promise you nothing will happen to you! May God be my witness!" She demonstratively raises her index finger in the air.

"Nobody can... ever... be proud of me! That's why... my mother also... died... Because of me... and my father... had to suffer... for a long time... A looooong time ... He suffered... his whole... life long... Because of me... But now... now... he no longer has to suffer... Now... he is... liberated... Yes... Nobody... has to suffer because of me... Nobody... can... ever... be proud.... of me..." Sam's weepy muttering is quiet, but clearly understandable to the three people standing below him. Hailey's tears roll quietly from her eyes and Stacy swallows a lump in her throat.

Angus briefly closes his eyes and takes a deep breath before speaking in a gentler tone, saying, "Come down now, boy! We can do it together!

I will count to three. If you don't jump then, I will go up and we'll jump together! Got it? One... two... three!!" No reaction, except for a pitiful sob, is heard in the stable. Resolutely the strong Scotsman walks over to the ladder and puts one foot after the other on the steps leading up to the loft.

"Angus! For heaven's sake! Don't do that!!! Sam! Please!" Hailey can't look. She turns around and buries her face in both hands.

Chapter 65

There is hectic confusion at the Conley house. Everyone is trying to keep a clear head and at least concentrate on who has to pack what and what the next steps are. Bonnie and Susie are ready with their suitcases and help Rosalía pack the twins' things. Ken has not yet unpacked his travel bag for the day and goes to the kitchen to make a snack for the twins to take with them. Roberto joins him to go over the details again.

Mirjam scurries around in excitement in her room and Linda carefully folds her clothes, placing them into the open suitcase. "Honey, you don't need that much, we won't be in Mexico long." Quietly, she puts a beige t-shirt back in the closet and watches her daughter take a gold necklace from the jewelry box. She stands next to her stand and put her hand on her shoulder. "That's pretty! I don't think I have ever seen it before! Did you get it as a gift?" Mirjam nods and says, "Skipper gave it to me... But it was always too valuable for me to wear it... If, we find her... I want to give it to her..."

***

Deep in thought, Frank closes the door to his study and walks through the now deserted room to his desk. He sits down on the comfortable leather armchair and opens the top drawer. From it, he extracts an unopened flask and a crystal glass. The room is silent except for the subtle clinking and pouring sounds. The smell of a clean-finished single malt wafts up to Franks nose and warms his lungs. He breathes it in, long and slow, then reaches down once more, this time to a second drawer, and pulls out a revolver. Setting the cold metal on the desk, Frank takes his glass in hand and makes a toast to himself, "Slàinte! To the headquarters! Better an end full of terror than an endless terror!"

Chapter 66

Hailey and Stacy's simultaneous loud scream makes the horses restless in their stalls. Sam awkwardly tries to get off the straw bales before Angus reaches the floor again via the wooden ladder. Of course, he didn't see the powerful push coming and had no idea how it happened. He notices a bad feeling that is slowly brewing in his stomach and wants to leave even faster than before. The alcohol level in his blood delays any movements he can make, and MacKay now stands next to him, wide stance and arms crossed. Sam is at a loss for what to do next. He notices that he is moving through the stable without using his feet. Only moments later does the stable boy feel the force with which Angus lifted him up by the collar of his shirt. He tries to fight back like a drowning beetle, but he can't get hold of Angus in any way.

"What are you doing with him?! Angus Cunningham MacKay?! Let him down! Let him go! Now this is really enough! Angus!! Sam!!" Hailey's unsuccessful scolding fades away like a dust cloud in the Scottish Highland wind. The two women watch as the big, strong Scotsman carries the skinny and defenseless boy in the air, over the gravel driveway, and drops him roughly in the blooming rose garden. He stomps over to the wall of the house and takes a long garden hose hanging there. He walks over to the heap of human wreckage lying on the ground, trying to pull himself up.

Before Hailey can reach the scene to protest, Sam feels the freezing cold jet of water blast the middle of his pale face. He gasps for breath and his green eyes turn into large marble balls. He starts screaming at Angus, "Please, please! Stop! Stooooop!!!! No, Angus! SIR!!! PLEASE, NO!!! Stop doing that!!!!"

"This is called a drunkard's shower! Do you understand?! Can you hear me?!" With tense shoulders and a stern expression, the land owner looks at the boy, who now appears to be sobering up, and is now trying to stand up but fails with every new jet of water blasted at him.

"Yes, yes! I can hear everything! Please stop it! SIR Angus!!!!" Sam's loud wailing is getting quieter and ends with a heartbreaking whimper, which spurs Stacy to action.

"That's enough now!" The veterinarian stands with her arms spread out between the threatening garden hose and the pile of human misery.

Angus raises an eyebrow and replies, "There is enough water for two..." After a brief but intense exchange of looks with the boy's defender, Angus slowly lowers the water weapon and looks past her.

"If you do that again, I'll use the pressure washer! You should get the same treatment as your old man!"

Chapter 67

"Tropman! Where's Tropman?!" The policeman rises from his chair and takes a bite of the sandwich in his hand. In the other hand, he is holding a telephone receiver, which he now places on his shoulder as he looks around the room. His colleague, who is sitting opposite him, raises his shoulders briefly and disinterestedly continues typing on his keyboard. "Has anyone seen Tropman?!" As soon as he has repeated the question, Tropman walks through the open office and lifts his head with interest.

"What do you have for me?" He walks over to the officer, who still has his mouth full, and takes the phone receiver off his shoulder. "This is Officer Tropman speaking!" He looks at his work colleague in surprise. "Frank Conley? No, I'm not ..." He speaks these words more softly and with more irritation, as he looks mysteriously around the room full of police officers. "Sure, I could do that... But what for?" Tropman frowns and purses his lips before murmuring an "OK" into the receiver and carefully placing it back on the phone base. "I'll be gone for a moment – it won't take long!" He walks past his colleague and hears from behind, "Take your time!" There is a loud laugh, which falls silent as he hurries down the fire stairs.

"What's up, Mister Conley? Long time since I last heard from you! It must have been about... ten? Twelve? ...years ago?" Playfully and casually, he leans back in his car seat and waits to hear Conley's voice from the radio loudspeaker. A deep, gentle laugh can be heard, followed by the voice of the former action hero, who says, "Ohhhh, Officer Tropman... What a clever cop you are, aren't you?!" Tropman frowns briefly and notices that beads of sweat have sprung up on his forehead. "What can I do for you, sir?" He brushes away the sweat with the back of his hand and swallows tightly.

"You seem tense, Officer! Are you having a hard day?" Frank's calm but provocative voice seems to be having an effect. Tropman opens the top two buttons of his shirt and loosens his tie. As if Frank were able to see this, he adds, "Constricting, isn't it?" Startled, the policeman looks around and takes a deep breath.

"Sir, if there's nothing I can do for you...."

"Oh, you can, Officer! You can do a lot for me! Why don't we just get straight to the point and start negotiating... Like, for example, how you could... let's say... give us back thirteen years and a baby?! How does that sound to you, officer? Shall we start with this... what YOU could do for me?!" Frank's voice is getting louder and more forceful, with an angry undertone. Tropman's sweat begins to increase dramatically and red spots appear on his neck. He tries to sound calm and matter-of-fact. "I don't know what you're talking about, sir? Was that all? I've got work to do!"

"I see... The police, your friend and helper in need, has a lot to do... Hmm... The question is, whose friend he is, am I not right, Officer?" Conley's voice has now taken on a sarcastic tone, which causes the policeman to tense every muscle in his body. He makes one last attempt to wriggle out of this uncomfortable situation in which he feels caught red-handed. He says, "Sir... I beg you for the last time..."

Chapter 68

Trembling, with his hair soaking wet, the hungover boy sits at the kitchen table. The smells wafting from the delicious food, which he usually tucks into heartily, are pressing his empty stomach menacingly higher and he hastily takes a sip of the broth that Hailey holds in front of his face. He grimaces in disgust and blinks, losing himself in shameful thoughts. When he hears Angus' loud, heavy footsteps in the hallway, he straightens his back and tries to put a concentrated expression on his face. He looks straight into the landlord's amused green eyes and notices the full glass of whisky in his hand. Hailey also seems to see this and stands close to Sam's side. "What are you going to do with that, Angus?!" She carefully puts a hand around Sam's shoulder and squeezes it gently.

"Are you a real Scotsman, Samuel Dunn?" Angus looks at his nervous assistant. Sam nods tentatively, not knowing what to expect next. But before the land owner can continue with the next lesson, Hailey intervenes again, saying, "No. Angus, that's out of the question! You leave the poor boy alone now…"

"Stop feeding him baby food?!" Angus interrupts his loyal companion and looks at Sam with a smile. "Is that what you want, Samuel? You want to keep being a Scottish baby? Or do you want to finally become a man and act like one, too!?" He walks around the table, slams the glass with the golden contents down in front of Sam, and hits him roughly on the back of the head.

"The best smell on a man is whisky! But YOU stink of cheap booze!!"

He goes back to the other side of the table and is about to leave the room when he hears the sound of Sam swallowing behind him. He smiles happily to himself and, without turning around, tries to speak with a serious tone, saying, "Make sure your stomach is filled with decent food, before you come out to the stable!"

"But Angus, let the boy recover from this horror and…" Hailey cannot finish her sentence once again when they hear Angus from the hallway, as he says, "His drinks?! Anyone who can drink can also work. And Abbey can't ride herself!"

Chapter 69

The loud bang from Tropman's car comes unexpectedly and makes him twitch. A shot, very clear to his trained policeman's ear. That was the sound of a shot just now. He looks around the car as if looking for a way to hold onto something and reaches for his cell phone, pressing it against his ear.

"Frank?! Frank Conley?! Can you hear me, damn it!?! Conley, answer me! Shit! Shit, shit... damn shit!!!!" He throws his phone on the passenger seat and bangs on the steering wheel firmly with both hands!

"You old bastard! You stupid old conceited Scot! You idiotic superstar!!! Shit, shit, shit!!!!" The policeman vigorously yanks the car door open and gets out. He leans on the car roof and breathes deeply in and out. He rests one hand on his hip and wipes the sweat off his forehead with the other sleeve. He then puts his hand on his mouth and looks into the empty car with his lips pressed together.

Thousands of lightning fast thoughts reach the thinking cells in his brain and he blinks hastily to try to classify each one somehow. What should he do next? He looks around as if he could find an answer on the street. The sweating of his body has now spread and is visible on his shirt. He tries again to wipe the cold sweat off his face and nervously pulls his tie over his head. After throwing it into the car, he looks at the entrance to the Coney Island police station and feels the urge to go inside.

But what then? Pretend nothing happened? Who knows about this phone call? Modlin only knows that Conley called him while he was on guard. There is not necessarily a connection. Also, the Hamptons have absolutely no connection with Coney Island. So the coincidence would have to be huge that any trace could lead to him. But who else knows what Conley knows? Maybe there's a farewell letter?

A racing car and squeaky braking tear him out of his thoughts about a cover-up plan. He looks

175

behind him and sees two men dressed in dark clothing getting out of an SUV and walking towards the entrance with long, fast steps.

Mayer and Cooper? Tropman's face gets even paler and his heart starts racing again.

He hears grating and rustling sounds from a distance and looks around in confusion. Slowly, he bends down and sticks his head into the noisy but empty car.

Chapter 70

Abbey is happy to have her new owner scrape out her hooves and enjoys the experienced hand movements. The large stable door opens slowly, and a bright strip of light floods the big wooden shed. Without looking up, Angus begins to speak. "I'm sorry...about your father..." When he hears footsteps coming towards him, he continues, "You don't just need strong arms and legs – you also need a particularly clear mind. The art of horseback riding is only a third of the skill. Your head is the other part." Slowly he runs his hand over the graceful white back of his mare and along her back leg down to her ankle. He clicks his tongue and is elegantly presented with the iron by Abbey. "And Abbey does the rest," he says, ending his theory lesson. He continues scraping out her hoof. After he has finished, he stands up slowly and looks into Sam's frightened eyes.

"But why do I have to ride? I've never done this before, and it is such an important performance for us tomorrow and... I can't do it..." Despondent and with sagging shoulders, the stable boy looks at the big horse and breathes noisily through his nose.

"I am not allowed to leave the property for a few days, so tomorrow you will do this for me! Miss Stacy and Hailey will be with you. And you're right, what you're doing tomorrow is important, so please pull yourself together! Now get Abbey's things and get her ready!" Angus puts the horse tools back in the box for them and lifts it off the floor. Sam looks at him in surprise and doesn't make a single move. "What do you mean, you are not allowed off the property, Sir?"

"They think I killed your old ...your father..." He tries not to look at the boy but notices out of the corner of his eye that the boy flinches briefly.

"But that's not true! Didn't you tell them that?" Sam shouts these words surprisingly loudly and energetically and Angus notices his clenched fists.

"Of course I did, my boy." The big Scotsman walks slowly past the slim boy, stops at his side and puts a calming hand on his trembling shoulder. "They say someone saw me. But don't worry – they can't harm us."

"Can't they?" The nervous stable boy looks sideways at Angus and swallows dryly.

"No, they can't because we haven't done anything wrong, Sam! Now go and get Abbey's things!" With an energetic hand gesture, he points him in the right direction and sets the door to the stall aside. He thoughtfully watches Sam walk slowly over to the materials room and crosses his arms over his chest. He fills his lungs with a deep breath and lets the air out noisily.

"Oh, Abbey! I hope this is the last MacKay stroke of fate..."

Chapter 71

Loud female screams and excited male voices appear to get into the interior of Tropman's car from afar. He now hears clear calls through his radio loudspeaker and hastily reaches for his cell phone on the passenger seat.

"Shit! It's still connected, damnit!" He has barely uttered these words and is about to press the button with his finger when he hears a deep, warm male voice clearly speaking from the phone, "Imaginary Scot? Nanana... tststs... Is that how you talk to an extremely idiotic superstar?" Frank Conley's voice resounds in a baritone through the inside of the car as if it were coming from another planet. The rest of the color now fades from Tropman's face and his trembling sweaty hands slowly lower the phone onto his lap.

"I'm a little disappointed, Officer... Well, what the hell... I'd like to have a chat with you. But listen to me. I have to calm my family down. The shot just sounded extremely loud... As you probably noticed... Oh man, and a terrible hole in my ceiling.... Other than that, I am certain that Mayer and Cooper have found their way to you in the meantime. Now it's time to settle the score, my friend! Hasta luego!" The loud crackling in the radio loudspeaker makes the frozen policeman twitch briefly.

Tropman's eyes slowly move up to the rearview mirror and his right hand reaches for the revolver in his holster. He gently takes it out and releases the safety. His eyes are still fixed on the entrance to the police station behind his car while he presses a speed dial button on his cell phone without looking. The loud ringing fills his car with noise until it is interrupted by a click, followed by an energetic whisper.

"What the hell?! Are you crazy?! You should never call me, except... Ahhh... Shit!!!!" The male voice with a Swiss accent stops speaking immediately and hangs up.

The two FBI agents run out of the building onto the sidewalk together and look from one side to the other. Cooper sees Tropman's car first and taps Mayer on the arm with his hand. "There! I think he's in there." Slowly the two agents, weapons drawn, walk towards the seemingly quiet car.

Cooper quickly opens the driver's door and curses loudly. "This can't be!! Damn it! Quick, call 911!"

Chapter 72

"Angus?! Call for you!" Hailey walks quickly and, as always, with short steps over to the training ground. She's holding an aging wireless phone and lifts it up in the air. Angus does not take his sight off of Sam sitting on the white, graceful mare and nods contentedly.

"Angus, are you listening to me? You have a call. It's a woman! Right here, look!" Excited and out of breath, Hailey holds out the device and blinks happily into the sun's rays. Angus takes a quick, scathing look at it and shakes his head barely noticeably. "I don't have time." He turns his attention back to the rider and purses his lips.

"Angus, you're just standing here! It is definitely important! Don't you even want to know who's calling?" Hailey waves happily, the phone still in her hand, and raises her eyebrows questioningly.

"Nope, I don't want to." Uninterested, he takes a few steps away from her and leans on the barrier again.

"Well then!" Hailey shrugs her shoulders and holds the receiver to her ear. To make sure Angus can hear her, she speaks loudly and exaggeratedly, stressing each syllable, saying "I'm sorry, Mrs. Graham, but Mr. MacKay has no time right now. You understand, just before the big day?! Yes, I'm really sorry... But I am sure you will find another property whose owners are willing to give a short interview for the NEWSPAPER... Yes... there are SOOO many great properties around here!" As she speaks this into the phone, she notices Angus slowly rocking his head back and forth. He tightens his back, extends his arm in her direction without looking and waves her over with his open hand.

"Oh, wait a moment, Mrs. Graham... I see he has found a minute for you! I hope you enjoy the tournament tomorrow! I'll be on the lookout for you so that we don't forget to take a picture!" With a radiant face, the small Scotswoman hands the old phone to Angus and claps her hands softly. She glances at Sam and Abbey and crosses herself, whispering "Protect our boy!"

In order not to avoid obviously eavesdropping on Angus, she takes a small pair of scissors from her lace apron pocket and cuts some flowers near the fence, holding them together in a bouquet. She bites her lower lip when she hears Angus say, "Of course, this is still MacKay clan family tradition and our young rider is Sam Dunn, my cousin."

Chapter 73

"Dad?! What was that?! Are you OK?!" Ken runs toward his father, followed by Linda and the limping Roberto. Jaws dropped and eyes wide open, they stand next to Conley Senior, who is sitting quietly, and Ken feels his chest. Roberto also goes over to him and grabs his wrist. But Frank waves both of them away, slowly stands up and walks over to Linda, who stands frozen, both hands covering her face. He slowly takes her hands off her face, opens her arms, and moves closer to her. He takes her head and puts it on his chest, hugs her around her shoulders and then only has to wait a few seconds to feel her sobs.

"Yes... That's right... I knew that had to get out..." He kisses her lovingly on the head and strokes her back gently. A gesture he made so often a long, long time ago.

"Frank? What's going on here?" Roberto looks from the two people hugging each other over at Ken, who is sitting on the chair, recovering from the first shock. He shrugs and also asks, "Dad? Was that just a shot?"

"Yes, my boy, that was a shot. A so-called 'start shot' for an old acquaintance of Linda's and mine." With these words, she moves away from Frank's arms, tears still running down her cheeks, and sniffs. She takes a handkerchief out of her capris pants pocket and dabs at the tears.

"Who do you mean?" She blinks at her former savior and now best friend.

"Do you remember the cop in Coney Island?" Frank puts both hands on her shoulders and looks at her closely. When she nods and frowns, he adds, "He will now lead us directly to your girl!" With determination and to give his statement more force, he squeezes her shoulders.

"No, he won't..." Susan Manders, who is still the best receptionist ever at Coney Island Hospital in New York, stands in the open door and lifts her cell phone into the air. Slowly, she takes it in both hands again and looks serious, saying, "I just got a call from Coney Island... Emergency..." With these words, a shiver goes through Linda's entire body and Frank immediately takes her tightly in his arms.

Susan walks into the room, sits on the leather couch near the wall and looks up at Frank. "Tropman gave himself the bullet..." Linda puts her hand over her mouth and looks up at Frank in horror.

"But... I don't understand..." Irritated, she waits for his reaction, which, to everyone's surprise, turns out to be very calm. He purses his lips and makes a slightly astonished sound, saying "Hmm... I wouldn't have thought that his remorse would be so big..."

"Dad?!?! How can you..." Horrified, Kenneth rises from the leather chair and walks over to Susie. He sits beside her and asks impatiently, "Did they say anything else?!"

Manders shakes her head and gives Frank a reproachful look.

Chapter 74

A police car slowly drives onto the gravel field through the driveway. The driver and passenger doors open, and Angus watches his old schoolmate step out.

"James, long time no see," he remarks sarcastically and raises his eyebrows in surprise when he recognizes the woman who has gotten out of the police car.

"And I see you brought an accomplice with you! M'lady!" Exaggeratedly and theatrically, he lowers his head in greeting and puts both hands in his pockets. The policeman glances at the woman, then walks over to the property owner.

"Hello Angus, so you know each other?" His question sounds more like a confirmation and he reaches to shake hands with Angus in greeting. Angus skillfully ignores this gesture and his gaze stays fixed on Stacy.

"To say that we know each other is an extremely overstatement, if I may say so!" He purses his lips and looks at the police officer with a smile, saying, "Inspection visit?"

"It depends on how you perceive it. Miss Rowan came to see me at station and testified for you. And I wanted to make sure that you knew each other... or whether she was a guest here that night."

Just then, Hailey and Sam walk out of the house. Sam is wearing beige breeches, an elegant dark green jacket and brown riding boots. Both look surprised to find the police and Stacy standing there but greet them politely.

"My dear, nice to see you here! Are you all right?" Hailey walks over to Stacy, interest and concern showing on her face at the same time, she takes Stacy's hand in both of hers. Looking coldly at the policeman, she asks, "James, do you need anything else from us?"

"No Miss Hailey, everything has just been cleared up. And I'm happy to see that MacKay will be represented there tomorrow. Hello Sam! I hope you're okay?" The relieved policeman waves to Sam and walks back to his car with determined steps.

"Do you want to go back to the village with me or will you stay here, Miss Rowan?" When he opens the driver's door, he gives her a questioning look and gets in shortly after, when he notices her look at Angus.

Chapter 75

One suitcase after the other is loaded into the black SUV in front of everyone. Frank hugs Mirjam warmly, saying, "Take care of your parents, Lassie! And see to it that Susie stays faithful to me and doesn't flirt with every single Mexican Muchacho she sees!" He laughs and kisses the teenage girl on the forehead.

"I will, Skipper! Even if I doubt that those men are her type!"

"Bleah, they will burn to a crisp under the Mexican sun before I get such an idea!" Susan walks energetically past the two and gives Frank a stern look.

"You know that I think that what you did was not OK!" Threateningly, she raises her finger and adds, "Even if he is now free of his feelings of guilt, YOU, my dear, have taken on new ones. You had no right to drive him into the corner like that! But the two gentlemen in suits will soon tell you that themselves!" She waves her hand over her shoulder to say goodbye and gets into the waiting limousine. "Hasta la vista, baby!"

"See you soon, my dears! And call me as soon as you get to the hotel!" Frank waves to his friends and watches the departing SUV.

Ken walks over and stands next to him, then grabs him by the shoulder, saying, "And you are sure that we shouldn't wait another day? You may need a lawyer after all, and Angus is off the hook for now. He got an alibi." Frank waves him away with his hand.

"No, you're going in advance. Bonnie has to go potty every five minutes out of sheer nervousness, and we can't make her wait any longer. I can manage quite well here on my own. Mayer is a good cop! We nail this Simon to the cross once and for all!"

The two tall men hug each other in farewell and are interrupted by the laughter of the youngsters. "Bye Baba! We're going on vacation again!" The twins each take one of their grandfather's legs and look up at him with joy.

"Oh yes, you are lucky! So go on, off with you into the cart!"

Rosalia hugs him too. "Don't do anything stupid! We'll need you in the Highlands soon, OK?"

As Bonnie walks out of the house and over to him to say goodbye, he opens his arms wide and embraces her. Surprised and embarrassed, she tries to free herself, but with no success. She snorts and says, "Let go of me, Frank! I can't breathe down here and you're crushing my hairstyle!" The big Scotsman laughs and lets go of her.

"You already sound like your sister! Come on now, get going!"

Chapter 76

Stacy breaks the silence at the table and looks at Angus, saying, "You seriously thought I was going to let you down?" When, as expected, no reaction comes from him, she picks up a piece of potato with her fork and spreads some butter on it with a knife.

"My dear, it was so incredibly brave of you to go to the police and testify! I am sure that Angus..." A loud bang interrupts them, scaring everyone except the person who caused it.

Angus rubs his hand, which he has just banged forcefully on the table. He looks angrily at his guest and snorts, saying, "What on earth came over you, thinking you can interfere in our family affairs?! You are not one of us, do you understand?! I have no idea what you're up to! But just because my ADOPTED sister changed your crappy diapers and taught you to speak doesn't give you the right to push yourself in here and play yourself up as a heroine! As soon as you swallow that last bite, you will leave my house, my property and our lives! You are no longer welcome at the MacKay house!"

He pulls the napkin off his lap, throws it on the table, moves his chair away from the table and goes to the door. Before he leaves the room, he stops and with his voice once again calm and matter-of-fact, he says, "Sam, you sleep in the blue room today. Don't drink too much so you can sleep well. I'll see you at four in the stable."

When they hear the door slam shut, they venture to breathe again. Stacy lets her tears run freely down her face, sobbing into her napkin. Hailey gets up quickly and walks over to comfort her. Sam sticks his fork into a piece of meat and directs it towards his mouth. Before pushing it in, he remarks with a mischievous smile, "He likes you a lot, Miss Stacy! He's just scared that you'll get into trouble too!"

Chapter 77

It takes longer than expected for the doorbell to ring. Without looking at the cameras, Frank opens the gates to the entrance and walks out through the front door. The black SUV with darkened bulletproof windows drives around the fountain that's surrounded by greenery and stops in front of the steps. The passenger door opens, and Cooper gets out, a serious expression on his face.

"Sir!" He nods his head briefly, walks up to Frank and extends his hand in greeting. Conley hesitates first, but then takes it, presses it tightly and returns the greeting. In the meantime, Mayer has also reached them and also shakes Frank's hand. He looks at Frank seriously, raising one eyebrow.

"You owe the government a police officer, sir!"

Frank lets go of Mayer's hand and leads the two men to the entrance. "Please, let's discuss the ugly details inside." He follows the two of them into the house and looks behind him suspiciously, albeit out of professional habit.

"Would you like some lemonade? My Bonnie makes the absolute best lemonade on the planet! And I can hardly offer you a whisky, can I?" Frank reaches for two tall glasses and pours the pale-yellow liquid from the carafe. As he hands Mayer the first glass, Mayer starts the discussion, saying, "Sir, your number was the last one on Tropman's call log. I assume you know what happened?" He takes a sip from the glass and nods in confirmation.

"I have no idea what happened, Agent Mayer! I swear! I called Tropman – you're right about that – but I had to say goodbye to my family. You see, the house is empty, everyone is gone!" He emphasizes his statement with his arms spread wide.

"Tropman shot himself...in his car! What did you talk to him about, Mister Conley?! We had an agreement!" A little more energetically, Cooper intervenes in the conversation and places his full glass on the table next to them. He puts both hands on his hips and continues, "Do you realize that he was our only key to finding Zimmermann?"

Frank sits down on a stool at the bar and takes a sip from his glass.

"Hmm..." He starts to answer thoughtfully, and continues, "If so, Agent Cooper, I wonder why even the FBI is lying to me?!" He takes another sip and looks questioningly at the two officers.

"I don't understand, "Mayer replies and walks over to Frank.

Frank points a finger at the other FBI agent and says, "Ask your friend here!"

Chapter 78

Sam, dressed for the competition, nervously paces back and forth in the stable. He shakes his head again and again and mumbles incomprehensible words to himself. A loud bang makes him jump and he runs out of the barn. In the dark light of dawn, he can only vaguely recognize something and hesitantly asks, "Angus?! Sir? Is that you?" He carefully takes a few steps further until the second, now clearly audible shot is fired!

"Angus Cunningham MacKay! You son of a bitch! I know what you did, and Conley won't be able to help you! No matter how much moolah he offers or how well known his face is! This is still Scotland and we cannot be bought! Where are you, you bastard!?" Another shot is fired and then Sam hears the heavy wooden door of the house opening. He still can't see anything, and yet the roaring voice sounds familiar. The rider stops, trembling and frozen waiting for another response in the gray dawn light. The lights from the bedrooms are bright and he recognizes Hailey standing by a window.

"What is this?! Don't you have anything better to do today?" Angus comes out of the house wearing corduroy pants and a knitted sweater. With both hands in his pockets, he walks calmly towards the visitor as if he were trying to calm a wild horse.

"Wait, that's right, you don't have a good horse to ride today... What a pity you couldn't buy Abbey. She'll win me the entire pot today... But you probably know that already... I didn't know that you were so well read and subscribed to the newspaper?!" He stops in front of the person holding the gun and Sam can now see that it's Ian MacDonald, his father's best and only friend.

"Listen." Angus slowly takes his hands out of his pockets and gets very close to the now snorting intruder. He grabs him by the jacket collar, looks down at him and whispers menacingly, "You should keep your fancies to yourself, otherwise things may go the same for you as they did for old Dunn. Now get the hell out of here! Otherwise I will be happy to drop by in a month with Conley tagging along! And you know that will not end well for you!" He gives the drunk man a push and looks over at Sam.

"All right, my boy! Sir MacDonald just wanted to make sure I am sending a qualified rider to the competition today!"

Chapter 79

"We won't get any farther like this, sir! What were you up to?" Mayer looks from Cooper to Frank and starts to continue speaking when a cell phone rings. Mayer looks at Cooper, who quickly reaches into his inside pocket, pulls out the noisy device and presses a button to switch it off. He sticks it back in his pocket, trying to make it look as if he is completely calm, and looks at the four eyes fixed on it. "Sorry, that's my private phone. I forgot to mute it."

Frank gets up and walks slowly over to the FBI agent. He stops short and looks at the man, who is almost as tall as he is.

"Perhaps you should order Zimmermann to come here right away and invite him to have a lemonade with us. I am very hospitable, as you should know." His ominous undertone prompts Mayer to approach the two and stand close to them. Cooper's hand slowly moves back to his jacket and Conley reacts, saying, "It would be best if you leave that alone, Agent. Why don't you just help us out of this damn mess and end it like a man!? With no dignity, of course... in your specific case!"

Mayer looks questioningly at his colleague. But before he can blink, Frank throws him on the floor, sits on his back and holds his arms crossed behind his back.

"Damn it! FBI! It's a wonder I'm not laughing my head off! And for all these years you've been fooling us all! Who else is behind this?" Frank Conley roars at the man below as a vein on his forehead threatens to burst.

Mayer has now grasped the situation and is standing with his legs apart, his gun pointed at Frank, who is next to him.

"Cooper?! Conley?! Damn it! What's going on here!? What is he talking about? Don't give me any shit. I don't want to pull the trigger! Let go of him slowly. Stand up, Conley, very slowly…!"

Frank doesn't move a millimeter but speaks menacingly at the man lying on the floor, "Come on, tell your loyal companion what's behind all this! And don't leave out a single detail! I have time and want to hear the whole story!"

Chapter 80

Sure of victory and yet a little wistful, Angus watches as the jeep and horse trailer drive out of the yard. Hailey's hand waves excitedly out of the open passenger window and Sam toots the horn to say goodbye.

"Stupid boy! You'll just make Abbey even more nervous!" The lord of the manor swears to himself, but then waves back briefly. He turns and walks towards the stables. He takes the halter and reaches for the saddle. A ride to the cliffs would do him good and Aaron is probably longing for a ride too. Their time together was far too brief, and Angus has a lot to tell him. In particular, this whole thing with Stacy isn't giving him the peace he hoped for.

Did he deal with her too harshly? He shakes his head. Now the competition is the focus and nothing else! That is exactly why those kinds of issues with women are not for him. They only distract you from what is important and lead you nowhere, except... well... maybe to a family. But who needs a family if they are all as screwed as like this one! And it looks like that won't be getting any better anytime soon, at least not until the matter with the mysterious fall has subsided.

Angus goes over to his stallion and throws the saddle on his back. "Women! Right, my boy? They only cause trouble! What was she thinking?!"

He ties the girth and is about to tie the reins when he hears a noise that cannot have been triggered without outside influence. He sticks his head out of the horse stall and looks straight into the veterinarian's beautiful eyes.

"This woman thought we should clarify this in private." She takes a step towards the stunned Scotsman and puts a hand on the stallion. She takes advantage of his surprise and pushes him back a little further into the stall, all the while keeping her gaze and her hand on the beautiful animal.

"You won't get rid of me that easily, you stubborn bull!" For the first time since they first met, she looks over at him with a look in her eyes that Angus Cunningham MacKay cannot classify, which makes him nervous and insecure.

Chapter 81

Frank Conley takes the vibrating Blackberry out of his pocket and takes the call. "Hey, my boy. Where are you?" He nods absentmindedly. "Yes, they were here.... Everything was fine... No, no incidents... As soon as Mayer informs me, I will inform Linda and Rob. That should only take a few minutes. The situation is about to explode... Of course not! We'll all come soon; I promise! Give Bonnie and the twins a kiss from me! Of course, Rosa too! Have a good flight, my boy!" He presses the key and looks at the man sitting in front of him in the chair.

He shakes his head and says to him, "There is a Scottish saying, 'Buy a thief from the gallows and he'll help you hang yourself!' They'll be slaughtered in the open, Cooper... But I think you already know this! No money in the world can buy out your shitty feeling now, can it? Was it really worth it? You couldn't even spend the damn money?! Or what did you do with it? Buy a villa in the Bahamas for a well-deserved retirement?!" He kicks his chair as if this would make the agent, whose hands are bound, talk. Mayer comes back into the room and looks at his long-time colleague with disappointment.

However, he speaks to Conley first, saying, "We know where he is!" And to his colleague, "Damn it, Cooper, really!? What were you thinking? How many babies were there? No, I don't even want to know! Not yet! I have to try to restore at least a small part of our honor... Damn! Shit on honor, shit on you, Cooper... I thought I knew you…"

He spits contemptuously at the criminal agent's feet and turns back to Conley, saying, "Sorry, that was a reflex and extremely unprofessional. I'll wipe that up right away. Call Mrs. Steiner now. Linda.

I have to talk to her!" His sharp tone tells Frank that his words to Ken were not exaggerated and he feels the chains that have been knotted up inside his chest for years beginning to loosen.

"Lassie, put mama on the phone! Now, Mirjam... It's urgent! No, she shouldn't check into the hotel! She has to answer the phone NOW!"

"Mrs. Steiner? FBI Agent Mayer on the phone. Where exactly are you?"

Chapter 82

Angus sits thoughtfully in his armchair in front of the blazing fire and waves his whisky glass. He smiles briefly, then clears his throat and takes a sip from the glass. The loud crunch from the gravel yard catches his attention and he gets up immediately. He steps quickly out of the living room, goes out the door and stops on the lowest step. The Jeep drives past him and over to the stables, as he throws his arms up in the air.

"Stupid boy! Where are your manners!" He quickly walks behind the horse trailer and straight towards the driver's door once the vehicle stops. He opens the door and looks expectantly at the boy behind the wheel. For a brief moment, they look at each other silently, Then Sam grins happily and holds up a silk ribbon with a shiny medal on it with his left hand.

The strong Scotsman pulls his cousin out of the Jeep and holds him up in the air by his jacket. "You did it!!! I'm proud of you, you scrawny skeleton!" He drops him roughly on the feet and hugs him briefly but so violently that it takes Sam's breath away for a second. He looks happily at Angus and nods sheepishly.

"Thank you, Angus... Sir! That means the world to me! But I didn't do it all on my own. Abbey was great, she..." He looks around proudly and notices Hailey moving slowly towards the two, with a serious look on her face. He leaves his unfinished sentence hanging in the air and looks at the small Scottish woman, who is now standing in front of Angus. Before he can greet her, she slams her handbag into his side.

"Ow!!! What was that for?!" Angus takes a big step away from her and puts his hand on the spot she just hit.

With a hissing tone to her voice, she answers his question, saying, "Do you think it's not shameful enough without you being there?! No, I had to listen several people, including someone from the newspaper, ask whether the oh-so-large and one-of -a-kind Angus Cunningham McKay with his winning horse Abbey would be too high and mighty to pick up the ringing phone and be informed about his win! Do you think that's a pleasant thing to go through?! Have I really spoiled and ruined you so much that you are too fine to take a receiver off the hook?!" She is about to hit him with her handbag again, when a loving voice behind her stops her.

"Miss Burns! Don't hit him, please! I am very sorry! This is all my fault! He couldn't take the phone call because of me…"

Chapter 83

The oppressive heat in Mexico makes large sweat beads break out of the pores of all three passengers. They sit in the back seat of the taxi in silence, nervous and tense. Mirjam, who is sitting in the middle, tries to imagine what will happen in this first encounter. She still cannot believe what has happened in the last 48 hours of her young life. How everything that was normal until now will never be the same. She has a sister... Or is she a half-sister? What would you call their relationship? Actually, she herself is the adopted child... But also not officially adopted... No, everyone believes that she is the biological daughter of Linda and Roberto... It is even on her birth certificate... She blinks violently and looks first from her father on one side of her and then at her mother on the other.

Linda looks tensely out of the window and lets the breeze dance on her face. She rubs her wet hands together and tries to make a little serenity flow into her body through finger pressure. Her heart is pounding so wildly that she feels it in her throat. She inhales and exhales deeply, which does not relieve the oppressive feeling in her chest. How was it that they never found out through all these years? Years of searching and trust have all been for nothing. And it doesn't take her daughter more than five minutes to bring everything to the surface. She has failed. Failed miserably as a mother. She tries to suppress the tears, but realizes from her daughter's soothing caresses that she has already been caught out in her emotional chaos.

Roberto's suppressed anger threatens to jump out of his body through his rocking leg. After all these years of physical and mental pain, is this the moment for the encounter to finally take place? He shakes his head. No, he still doesn't dare to believe that he will see Simon and look into his malicious eyes. The last time he saw his admirer, he himself was lying on the stretcher in the ambulance and was being taken to the madhouse as a half-burned, insane suicidal cripple. Simon's last words had been, "We are always close by!" This was supposed have a calming effect on him. At the thought, a shiver runs through him and makes him flinch. He was so close to her. He had heard Mirjam crying through the open window of Simon's car. He was so close on their heels... And then... That truck carrying a full load of oil...

"Are you all right, Papa?!" Mirjam hugs him lovingly but doesn't take her other hand off her mother.

"I wonder if she's still called Mirjam." The teenage girl speaks her thoughts out loud but doesn't expect an answer.

Chapter 84

The look on Hailey's face and her confused gestures make Sam's face break out in a broad, mischievous grin. With a swipe from Angus, he immediately forces the grin off his face, clears his throat and resists the temptation to smile again by looking down. Stacy looks expectantly at Hailey and takes another step towards her.

"My dear, how nice to see you here! But... your hair is completely wet! I don't understand... Is everything alright with you!? What happened then!?

Why are you to blame for Angus not answering the phone? Angus!? Do you want to tell me what's going on here?! What did you do to Stacy?! Angus Cunning-!!!" Hailey starts to walk over to Angus, speaking in an energetic tone, when Stacy steps in between them.

"Everything is fine, Miss Burns! Angus did nothing to me. On the contrary, he forgave me! Isn't that right, Angus?" She looks over her shoulder and notices the two men trying to pull themselves together and stay serious. Angus nods slowly, holding his hand over his mouth as if he has to think about it seriously. Hailey cannot have realized that this is just a way to stop himself from grinning.

"Ohh!! Is this really true?! What a great day it is today!" She squeezes Stacy's hands and then touches her wet hair. "Did you get dirty, my dear?" Stacy gives her a smile and replies, "Angus let me help in the stable, as reparation, so to speak. And then we forgot the time and didn't hear the phone... I'm really sorry, Miss Burns, really! We should install another telephone in the barn in the future so that this won't happen again!"

"We?! In the future?! Oh dear! It almost sounds as if you are going to accept Angus' offer after all and stay with us at the manor?!" Hailey's sparkling eyes look as if they are ready to jump out of her face as she says out loud what she has finally realized She claps her hands and looks proudly at her protégé.

"I knew you were a good boy and would make me happy one day! I'm so proud of both of you!" She looks alternately from Angus to Sam, both of whom are now looking around the table, rather perplexed.

Chapter 85

Frank paces restlessly in the kitchen. He opens a cupboard, takes out a bowl and places it on the table. He opens the next cupboard door and reaches for a box of colored balls. He then empties the contents, into the bowl. He takes the bottle of milk from the fridge and gives the door a kick to close it. After filling the bowl to the brim, he quickly dips a spoon into it and stuffs the unhealthy comfort food into his mouth. He has just taken the first noisy bites when the phone rings. Still chewing, he hastily reaches for the receiver and makes an incomprehensible sound.

"Frank? Was that you?! Holy smokes, can't they even get a decent connection here?! Hey! Amigo, I think your phone is broken!" Susie's familiar voice calms Conley's nerves a bit and he swallows the bite of food.

"That was me, Susie! I'm calming my stomach a little with Froot Loops, sorry!" Her hearty loud laugh puts a smile on his tense face.

"You will soon need my old stretch pants, boyfriend, if you let yourself go like this!" She doesn't wait for his reply, but continues speaking immediately, "They are on their way to the border guard. All three of them. And I don't have any power on my cell phone, which is why I am standing in at the counter of a small tequila bar, just behind the madhouse. You cannot imagine what is going on there, Frank. Susie would like to throw her erotic curves at the tiny, bald potbellied pig and wring his neck! Unfortunately, I am no longer allowed to enter.

212

Everything is cordoned off and surrounded by police officers. I bet they brought all the uniformed forces from the countryside here! Caramba, this is a sight to see. The counter here is full! He will be making one hell of a profit today, I tell you - Amigo! Un tequila para la señora, por favor! - Excuse me, sweetie, but this thrilling spectacle is better than all of your movies put together!" Manders speaks so hastily and excitedly that she hardly gets a breath of air between her sentences.

Conley presses the receiver firmly to his ear and slowly sits down on a bar stool, pushes the cereal bowl aside and puts his forehead in his hand. He closes his eyes and listens as big, imaginary chains are broken in his chest.

Chapter 86

Angus has just driven the stylish Cadillac out of the garage when Hailey waves at him to stop. She shakes her head and walks towards the car. Angus winds the window down and looks at her questioningly.

213

"Delay. The plane is late, my boy! They can't leave Glasgow because of the wind... Not yet, anyway... But soon...and...the Cadillac will not be enough..." Embarrassed, she traces the window pane with her finger. Angus briefly closes his eyes and asks, "How many?"

The petite Scotswoman raises one hand and spreads all five fingers apart. Before he can comment, however, she whispers, "For the moment..."

A few minutes later, the spacious VW bus rolls out of the shed and Sam emerges from the stable. "Oh yes, right, Frank Conley is coming today! I can't believe I will meet him in person! I will meet him, won't I?" Excited, the new MacKay horseback rider approaches the bus and waits for the driver's door to open.

"No, you will not!"

"But ... I don't understand... Won't he be staying with us... I mean... here, with you?" Curious, he follows his boss and cousin to the stable.

214

"The old man isn't coming today. And if it were up to me, he could stay in Hollywood!"

"New York, Angus, he lives in New York! And I wish you wouldn't talk about him so disparagingly! He is a member of our family, as is Sam. And you know perfectly well that it wasn't his fault!" At first factually, then very emotionally, Hailey is still trying to smooth the waves after all these years. She looks sadly at Sam.

"You know that, don't you, my Sam? Our Frank was not to blame for this terrible accident! And he most certainly did not take Heather from us! So ridiculous!"

The stable boy looks at Angus and then down at his feet. "My father used to say she sacrificed herself for the MacKay clan... She only married this Conley so you would be fine with the money... And then in America she was killed in cold blood by her drunk husband..." Ashamed, he looks up at Angus and sees a human explosion about to take place immediately after his last word.

Wooden barrels are thrown through the air, a pitchfork is thrown through the stable with full force, halters are torn off the hooks and a large wooden door is taken off its hinges to be flung away as well.

"STOOOP!!!!" A loudly screeching woman's voice makes the angry Scotsman pause. Taking a deep breath and exhaling, he looks angrily around him. He looks straight into Stacy's lovely eyes, which fill with tears.

"Angus, no!!! Don't! Stop doing that!!! You know that's not true! And I know it too! Heather was in love! Head over heels and with her whole heart, she was crazy about Frank Conley! Finally a man who was sincere with her and was good to her! He always supported her and never used her like the others! Not a day, hardly a minute passed without her thinking about him or you! About him because she could not imagine living without him... And, about you... How she would ever have the heart to leave you here alone!" Slowly and with both hands in the air, as if she had to protect herself from the unforeseen, the new MacKay houseguest approaches Angus, who is still holding the door in his hand and letting his lungs breathe more slowly.

"She had to get out of here, you know that! Away from all the shame, that Ian brought upon her!"

Chapter 87

The large iron door opens as if by magic and the three visitors enter slowly and hesitantly.

"Señora Steiner, Señor Garreffa, Señorita." The small border policeman approaches the Swiss family seriously and only shakes hands with Roberto. He sort of nods in greeting to the two women and points with one hand, saying, "Por favor." He leads the way through a cold labyrinth of old, white walls and even older doors. The place looks run down and shabby, which underscores the offensive fragrance in the air.

Mirjam takes her mother's sweaty hand and walks silently next to her, her own hear pounding. She is not yet sure what to expect, but she can tell from her father's reaction that it is very serious. She has never seen him like this before. Tense, full of rage and bitter anger in his eyes, and yet a wistful and sad look also. She has definitely never seen her mother like this. She has been cold and withdrawn since the day they went to take her blood samples. It was as if her mother had retreated into her shell like a turtle, waiting for a wasp to whiz by.

They walk through the last door at the end of the corridor, past a water cooler. Mirjam tugs her mother's hand briefly. "Mom may I, please?" She points to the water and they stop. The cool water does all three of them good, distracting them for a moment, and Roberto opens the top buttons of his shirt.

In fluent but very broken English, the Mexican policeman remarks, "They were separated as soon as we brought them here..." He cannot continue speaking. The people following him stop and as if they have agreed in advance, the married couple replies in one voice, "They?!"

The policeman also stops and nods. "Sí, father and daughter! Who did you expect to find here??!"

Chapter 88

The aging but well-maintained VW bus drives over the bumpy stone streets of the Scottish Highlands. Angus holds his right elbow out of the window and casually steers the large steering wheel with this hand. He holds his left firmly on the stick shift and nods his head slightly to the music coming out of the old radio. Sam, who is sitting next to him, stares at Angus, also nodding his head to the music and thinks that he has never seen the laird of the manor in such a good mood.

Something has changed in the past few days. He hardly dares to think back to that night. On the one hand, because it was the last time he spoke to his father. On the other hand, because Angus made it clear to him that this matter should be based on himself. An accident. Yes, it was an accident. One that could have been prevented... But at what price? Who is this mysterious witness? That Ian guy? But how and where could he have watched them? No one except Angus and he himself knows this crash site. No, not even his father knew where he was stepping.

"I'm not your type! So stare at the street and not at me. That's rude!" Angus hits the boy gently with his fist and grins. "And if you do that with the old Conley, I will personally put you in the loony bin! We have had a lot of issues in the family, but insanity is not yet one of them!"

"Angus?" Sam tries desperately not to take his eyes off the road. When he doesn't get an answer, he continues, "Who saw us?"

The strong Scotsman calmly drives the VW bus in the direction of the airport and replies, "Nobody! The stupid show-off Ian was drinking with your father before he came over to challenge me. When he didn't return, his drinking buddy knew that something must have happened to him. And that was good. Otherwise the animals would have caught him before the police."

A cold shiver runs through Sam and Angus looks at him, saying, "Hey! WE have done nothing wrong! Is that clear? Listen to me carefully! It was time for him to pay for his bullshit! Enough was enough! And if you drink yourself stupid and make life hell for everyone, there's a faster way! What did he want to prove?! Did he want to challenge me to see if I would watch him punch you over and over and beat you to death?! Out of pure fatherly love?! The way he ended your mother's life?! Just like he and Ian chased my sister to the city, then out of the country?!"

Chapter 89

"Señor Garreffa, you are now allowed to go in, accompanied by a policeman. I don't know what contacts you have, but there has never been anything like it in my entire career. But no sé what or who is behind it!"

Hoping for an explanation, the border policeman looks up at Roberto, who is staring intently at the door in front of them. He pays no attention to the little man in front of him but looks back briefly at Linda and Mirjam to get emotional support from their faces. He closes his eyes briefly, tightens his shoulders and nods to his companion.

He has barely taken two steps into the smelly room and exchanged the first silent eye contact when his stomach turns. He holds his hand over his mouth, but cannot hold it back, he just manages to turn to the wall splatter the contents of his stomach on it.

"Roberto?!" The familiar male voice behind him again once again threatens to make him vomit.

"Señor Garreffa, por favor! Señor, please, come back with me!" The door is torn open forcefully and Roberto is pushed through with his upper body still hunched over.

"Papa?! What happened?!" Mirjam immediately runs over to her coughing father and her eyes meet the green eyes in the room for two seconds. The door closes again immediately, but Mirjam remains frozen and thick tears start to roll down her tender, youthful cheeks.

Linda also grabs her husband under his shoulders and together they help him walk over to the nearest seat. Roberto leans both forearms on his thighs and sips the mug of cool water. The policeman who was supposed to accompany him now hands him a cool, wet cloth and puts both hands on his hips.

"Dios mío, Señor! He doesn't look that bad, this American! The girl is prettier, I have to admit. Do you want to see her first?"

And before he can show his silver tooth in a smile, he is slammed to the ground with full force.

Chapter 90

The two women sit silently in the spacious kitchen, preparing the fresh garden vegetables in front of them. Warm bagpipe sounds can be heard from the nostalgic radio with its antenna and the head swinging back and forth tells Stacy that this is quite suited to Hailey's taste in music. She notices that she is being watched and smiles with satisfaction.

"It's beautiful, isn't it, my love? Back then my father always played for us girls. We danced and sang Gaelic songs. Bonnie had such a wonderful voice... And..." Her eyes fill with tears, which she instantly conjures away with a smile. "Yes, Rose, she danced like an angel! She was the oldest of the three of us." She shakes her head. "The prettiest, the smartest and the wildest!" Hailey laughs out loud as if she has remembered a funny story.

"Oh...my dear!!! She was so wild! And fearless!" Now with a sad look on her face, she takes another potato and peels it expertly. "That was her undoing, you know... That terrible, cruel war... Oh my dear... How terrible it was here in Scotland at that time..."

Stacy looks at the now very thoughtful, delicate and downright fragile woman next to her. She observes how she swallows hard and watches a tear creep slowly down her flushed cheek.

"You don't have to tell me about it anymore, Miss Hailey, that's fine. It is such a wonderful day today and it will get even more beautiful!" She puts down her paring knife, wipes her hands on a towel, and starts to put one hand on Hailey's shoulder when

Hailey nods vigorously and looks at Stacy with determination.

"No, my dear! I do want to tell you! Don't you understand?! My good boy... Angus, he had to see so many bad things..." She also puts her knife aside and wipes her hands on her apron.

Stacy smiles lovingly at her and hugs her.

"But I understand, Miss Hailey! Heather told me a lot of secrets. Also that Angus found her when Ian and Dunn..."

Chapter 91

Excited, as if he has to audition for a million-dollar role, Frank Conley paces up and down in his study. He holds the phone tightly to his ear as he listens to Susie's report and nods periodically. Suddenly, he stops, slowly sits down on the closest chair and leans back. He slowly closes his eyes and a satisfied smile flits across his face.

"Thank you Susie, thank you! No, you shouldn't do it now, otherwise you may go straight to jail with them... I know, I know... It's the same with me... But they're actually much worse off now than if we had settled with them... Yes, I'm sure of it! I wonder if the psycho will be extradited to the States... He's American, isn't he? And Simon returning to Switzerland? That would not be so good. They certainly spoil the criminals in jail there... Yes, that's right! You could be right! What's going on?! Susan?! Hello?! I can't hear you anymore! Who is screaming? What has happened?! Hellooo??!!"

In a flash, Conley rises and looks around the room nervously. He takes a quick look at the phone, immediately puts it back to his ear and tries his luck again. "Susie, are you still there??!!" As if he could drown out the loud noises on the other side of the line, he calls out loudly into the receiver, "Helllooo!!!???" He angrily throws the device onto the sofa and walks quickly out of the room. He goes into the kitchen and takes his Blackberry off the counter.

"Crap!" As he looks at his display, he notices two missed calls. Agent Mayer and Ken. He closes his eyes for a split second, opens them shortly afterwards, purses his lips and nods resolutely.

"First thing first!!" With these words, he taps the redial key and waits for the call to be answered.

He hears loud screeching and funny laughter. Frank's face takes on a satisfied expression again. He hears his son's familiar voice saying, "Hey Dad! As you can hear, we are already on the Highland roads. The children think that they are even better here than in Mexico!" Once again, he hears the joyful childish voices of his two grandchildren and Frank also has to laugh out loud at the scene he is imagining. When he hears a deep male voice with a Scottish accent in the background, a queasy feeling begins to spread in his stomach area.

"Angus..." He mumbles more words to himself that he really wants to say out loud.

"Yes, Dad, Angus picked us up in a really cool VW bus! The poor man; these kids are going to give him PTSD!" Ken laughs cheerfully and Frank sees in his mind's eye the wonderful times they had in that very VW bus.

227

"What's wrong with that guy?! I don't have to put up with that! Not from a runaway tourist! Caramba! Mierda!"

The Mexican man, bleeding from his nose, holds a cloth up to his face as he continues swearing. He puts his feet on the table in front of him and alternately looks up from the bloody cloth to his colleague. "What's this shit all about?! Why are they allowed to go to see prisoners anyway?! What kind of riffraff are they?! And what language do they speak? Can I lock him up right away? Damn bastard!"

"No, you can't... I don't know what exactly is going on... Order from above. Why did you have to make a remark like that? Keep something like that to yourself it will cause you even more trouble and doesn't belong here! Now go, wash yourself and change your clothes. Then you stay behind. I will take her to the girl now when the father has calmed down again. He's going to keep puking all over the place..." Shaking his head, the senior policeman of the

Mexican border guard walks out of the room and lets the door close behind him.

"Señor? Are you feeling better?" He takes a respectful step towards Roberto and puts his hands on his hips. His question is answered by Linda, who is sitting next to Roberto. "He's getting better, thank you very much! Sorry for the inconvenience. I think it will be better if my husband stays here and calms down a bit and I go inside." Roberto and Mirjam jerk in surprise as they look at her from the side.

"But Mama, what if he does something to you again? I don't want you to go in there alone! Papa, right? She shouldn't do that!" Mirjam grabs her mother by the arm as if this would change her mind. Terrified, she looks at Roberto. He looks at his wife's determined expression, then says, "She will do it much better than I could, my darling. It's OK. Nothing will happen to her here. This nice policeman won't take his eyes off her for a second. Am I right, Señor?" He looks up questioningly at the policeman, who tightens his chest and instinctively puts his hand on the revolver in his holster.

229

"Pero sí, Señor! Of course I will be with her every step of the way." And then turning to Linda, he asks, "Are you ready?"

She looks at her worried daughter, gives her an encouraging wink and puts a hand on the scarred half of her husband's face.

"He will never be able to do anything to us again!"

Chapter 93

"Would you like to have children, my dear?" Without looking up from her the preparation work that she has resumed, Hailey asks this obvious question. Stacy stops slicing vegetables for a moment in surprise and looks at the tiny wrinkled woman next to her. Since no reaction comes, she continues chopping the potatoes and nods.

"Yes, gladly, if that's the destiny that is meant for me." Apparently, this is the desired and correct answer because Hailey nods contentedly and smiles.

"That is the right attitude, my dear. That's wonderful. You know, you can never be sure of what plans our Lord in Heaven has for us. Sometimes He gives us children, sometimes not. Sometimes He gives us children and then takes them away again." After this statement, she inhales air through her nose and then wipes it with her handkerchief. Stacy puts down her paring knife and walks over to the small Scotswoman. She puts her arm comfortingly around the shoulder and gently hugs her.

"And we will never understand why He can be so generous and loving on the one hand, and so cruel on the other, right?" Both women look out of the window into the courtyard and watch the horses in the nearby pasture.

"Did you want to have children, Miss Hailey?" Stacy dares to speak her question hesitantly. She inhales through her nose and feels the woman in her arms tighten her shoulders and stretch her back. She shakes her head barely noticeably and moves away from Stacy. Wiping her hands on her apron, Hailey attempts a smile.

"Now let's get back to work! Our guests will arrive soon, and the soup is not even on the stove! What will Kenneth think of us baboons! Oh, he's such a good and hardworking boy, our Kenneth!"

During this abrupt change of subject, she begins to whirl around chaotically in the kitchen. "He is a professor, have I told you that? Law Sciences! And a good prosecutor too! He's just like our Heather. You will see, he also looks like her. He turned into such a handsome, smart, and good man!"

The veterinarian listens to her carefully and observes her every move. She will speak to Angus about this sometime. Even if this thought initially makes her uncomfortable when she remembers all the cruel stories of this clan. Lost in thought, she looks around the kitchen and wonders what stories these walls could tell. Suddenly, Hailey grabs her by the hand.

"My dear! Didn't you hear me?! They are here!"

Chapter 94

Frank walks quickly up the curved staircase to his bedroom. Meanwhile, he taps the redial button and the speaker on his Blackberry. The ringing echoes loudly in the stairwell and is interrupted by a male voice.

"Mayer!"

"Conley here, what's going on down there?! I can't reach anyone!" Excited, the former action hero goes to his dressing room and carelessly throws clothes into a large leather bag.

"The media got wind of things and sent vultures to the clinic. There was a huge commotion, as you can imagine. The first strikes have already started, and a raging pack of human rights defenders is walking around the village. You were able to stop Mrs. Manders in time. Not to her satisfaction, of course. She would have liked to get even more mixed up in everything. Not an easy lady, your friend!"

Although Frank, who has just been interrogated, feels pressured and wrinkles his forehead, he has to smile at the FBI agent's remarks.

"Do they have them all?" Frank Conley stops for a moment, grabs a sweater and looks at the small cell phone on his bed. He hears loud screams and roars in the background and the loud sirens from police cars. The FBI appears to be following the entire thing live.

"Every single one of them taken, sir! From the top floor to the high-quality day care center!" His sarcastic tone causes Frank to let out a loud shout. For the first time in a long while, Frank takes a deep breath and closes his eyes.

"If there is a God, this would be the first moment in this story to thank Him, right? I thank You from the bottom of my heart!" Conley folds his hands in prayer and looks out of the window, out at the ocean under the open sky.

"What's next, Mayer?"

Chapter 95

Holding both hands over her mouth and nose and with tears in her eyes, Hailey looks at the VW bus parked in front of the guest house. Her legs feel stiff and paralyzed, but Stacy puts her arms around her shoulders and gently leads her down the stairs, then across the gravel yard. As soon as the driver's door opens, Ken gets out on the other side. Otherwise there is no movement to be seen or heard. Hailey takes her hands from her face in surprise and walks hesitantly towards the parked bus.

"Auntie Hailey!!!" With a beaming look and outstretched arms, the tall, young man goes over to the still confused woman and starts to hug her.

"But... where is everyone else?" She starts to go past her nephew over to the bus when she is stopped verbally and with a wave of her hand by Angus, who says, "Shhh! Don't wake them up now!"

"Everyone's here, Aunty! The boys have finally fallen asleep and Rosalía and Bonnie are serving as their pillows. I think those two are also taking a nap..." Conley Junior looks at his uncle, amused, and shrugs his shoulders.

"Do I get a Scottish hug now or do I have to be knighted first?" He turns happily back to his great aunt.

"Oh my boy, excuse me! I was so happy to see all of you that it took my breath away for a moment. Of course, come here! Let me take a look at you!" Hailey hugs her tall grandnephew, who has to bend over to get down to her level, as he lifts her into the air. "Let me down! You don't do that with a lady from the Highlands!" Laughing, she slaps him on the upper arm and adds, "You are also far too thin! I need to talk to my sister about her cooking skills now! Rubbish – they don't need to sleep! The children will get enough relaxation and fresh air here! Unlike in your stinky big city! Get out of my way, Kenneth!"

Angus rolls his eyes and opens the back area of the bus, saying, "Well, then let's stop being quiet. Sam, get out and help me with the luggage!" He glances over his shoulder at Stacy, who is standing there looking a bit lost, nods and winks at her.

"M'lady!"

Chapter 96

The border policeman carefully opens the door as if to prevent another disaster. He takes a quick glance into the room, then nods and opens the door completely. While Linda is now able to see the entire room, her Mexican helper does not take his eyes off her. Her cheekbones tremble with tension, but her gaze does not show any emotion. Appearing calm, she walks slowly and elegantly towards the table in the middle of the room and sits down on the empty chair. Her gaze does not deviate from the person sitting across from her, who examines her closely. They look at each other in silence for a long time until Simon breaks the silence, saying, "Hello Jasmin. You are looking good! The mother role seems to suit you well!" A mischievous grin lets his snow-white teeth flash and his green eyes sparkle maliciously.

Linda's face still shows no reaction, as if she's waiting for more.

"Did your emergency rescuer teach you that? Your famous actor? What was his name? Unfortunately, I was too busy all those years to go to the cinema..." When he still does not get a reaction from her, he raises an eyebrow and loads more ammunition to target her with.

"How is YOUR Mirjam doing? She must have become a pretty young woman like her mom, that is... Um... Maybe it was... A funny story, Jasmin... I have to tell you..." He puts both hands on the table and leans over towards her slightly.

"I heard her crying when the little one was taken away from her and taken to the loony bin... It wasn't as quiet as it was in your hotel... But it was something completely different... Not really planned, I mean... And you were almost dead..." When he sees the tear that falls from Linda's eye onto her cheek, he stops in the middle of his sentence and leans back confidently in the chair.

"Hmm ... So, you're not that cool... I thought so, you know!" He raises his index finger as if he intends to reprimand her, continuing, "You have always acted braver than you actually were! Ms. University Professor!" He throws his head back and laughs mockingly.

"Listen, Jasmin, I don't know what game you are playing here or what you hoped for. Robbie just showed more class by throwing up on the floor. At least I know how he is feeling in this situation. And it was nice to see that the accident did not leave too many traces...at least externally..." He clears his throat and looks at the policeman standing in the room with his hands raised.

"Am I just supposed to look at this woman and tell her stories?! I think we're done here?! Can I see my daughter now!? She will be beside herself with fear. She is such a tender, shy being. I wonder who she got it from?"

Chapter 97

Kenneth walks slowly through the large, light-flooded stable and admires the stately horses. He walks up to a white, curious animal and gently puts his hand on the bridge of the horse's nose. He reads the name aloud from the wooden panel next to the stall opening. "So you're Abbey! We just heard great stories about you. Congratulations on your first success." As if the proud mare understands him, she shakes her noble head, making her magnificent mane dance. Ken laughs and replies, "Yes, you understand, don't you?"

"You should be careful what you say out loud in here." Angus walks past his lawyer, holding a large pitchfork, and opens Abbey's stall door.

"Can you ride, nephew?" He stands next to his winning mare and caresses her neck. "Come on, my lovely, I need some fresh air and a break." As asked, Abbey walks elegantly through the opening and, as a matter of course, in one direction. Astonished, Ken watches this and points at her.

"She is going by herself? But where is she going?"

"She is choosing a horse for you. You can follow her calmly – she has extraordinarily good taste." With a smile, Angus puts the pitchfork into the open stall and follows the other two.

"Angus, I have not yet thanked you for your generous hospitality! I know it is unusually loud and messy with the twins and my wife will keep you busy too. She couldn't wait to finally come here after all these years in which she has been dreaming of this country." He follows his mother's brother, who is only a few years older than himself, to a brown horse's head next to Abbey.

"Good choice, Abbey. May I introduce; Mad." The big Scotsman looks at his visitor with an amused look on his face.

"Oh, that sounds promising! Mad, I'm happy to explore the Highlands with you. Just let me live, I have a family."

"No worries, lawyer. 'Mad' is the abbreviation of 'Madison.' He's as tame as a lamb, aren't you, my old boy?" Angus lovingly opens the wooden door and lets his horse run out of the stall.

"I cannot believe that they can move around so freely here and know where to go! How do you do that, Angus?" Conley Junior walks alongside the laird and follows him over to the saddles.

"Are your children not allowed to run around freely at home? If they don't know the rules, you don't trust them... Or your upbringing is miserable!" The confident Scotsman looks out from behind a saddle and asks in a serious voice, "Do you trust me? Will you believe my version of the story??"

Chapter 98

Frank Conley casually swings the leather bag over his shoulder and briefly stumbles.

"Can't get your ass up so easily, eh Frank?" Amused, Mike takes a few steps towards his employer and friend. Frank raises his clenched fist in a threatening manner and replies, "Just make sure your' plane here doesn't wobble! My stomach has too much acid and is only filled with Froot Loops. That may be dangerous for you!" Barely at eye level with each other, both men laugh and hug each other briefly but warmly.

"Well then! Have you decided which way to take off?" The pilot takes the travel bag from his passenger's hand and carefully puts it under the back seat.

As Conley settles in the co-pilot's seat, he nods thoughtfully, replying, "We'll get Susie first. She is driving everyone crazy down there."

Mike laughs into the microphone. "Oh, I can picture it very clearly!" He pauses for a moment and adds something more serious and quieter, saying, "Did she meet Simon? Or the psychiatrist?" A dark veil flies over Mike's face as he frowns at the last questions and looks at Conley.

Frank shakes his head and looks at his pilot with understanding. "No, and it's better that way. However, she was able to observe the raid in the clinic with her own eyes and will tell you personally and in detail, I am sure, Mike! You will be done with it soon. The thing is over! It is finally time to let go."

With a caring yet determined look on his face, he grabs his friend by the shoulder and pats it. The latter nods his reply in silence and closes the plane door.

"What about Mirjam? So, I mean..." He puts on the headset and their conversation now continues via the microphones.

"You mean Linda's biological daughter... I've already asked if she's still called Mirjam... They are both at the border guard office. I don't know any more. As soon as we have Susan back with us, we will try to reach her. My dear Susan will tear me to pieces if I do it now without her, even if I can hardly stand waiting. But you can imagine what an explosive blast we are going to meet up with soon... Take off, buddy, she will be arriving at JFK any time now!"

Chapter 99

"Who is this Stacy Rowan standing in the yard? What is she doing?" Ken looks intently at the dark sea in front of them and tries to get all the facts together.

"She's a cow midwife." Angus also looks at the view he is so familiar with and then at his lawyer. When he sees Ken's forehead wrinkle, he takes his hand off the reins and clenches it into a fist. "Well, she sticks her fist or even her entire arm in the cow's rear and..." Angus' very clear description makes Conley Junior gasp and he immediately interrupts the Angus with his hand held up.

"She's a veterinarian?!" He grins at his uncle, who gives him a zealous wink. "Yes, that's what I just said! There's not much more to do up here for her. She still won't touch the horses around here, because we have our specialists." With these words, he gently pats Aaron's neck and swings his right leg over the horse's back. "My butt is as hard as old porridge! Driving a car is not for me, and I have no idea how you can endure this on the plane!"

"Well, then you have the best care on the farm. I wasn't born yesterday, and I also have eyes in my head. There's more to this alibi, isn't there?" Kenneth dismounts his horse, if not quite as elegantly as the Scott. He takes the reins in his hand and starts to follow Angus, who stops suddenly. The sounds of a

245

horse galloping are coming closer and getting louder. Both men look in the direction from which the sound of galloping is coming, and Angus' gaze hardens. Ken blinks and squints his eyes a little, hoping to be able to see more. "Who is that? What is going on? He's riding as if he were on the run!"

"He probably is. That's Sam. And this means trouble..." Disappointed to have to interrupt his break, the laird of the manor swings back onto his stallion's saddle and takes the reins for a moment. His nephew does the same and settles himself on the saddle.

"Angus!!! Quick!! You have to go back! Ian and this policeman..." Out of breath, the stable boy stops in front of the two and tries to calm his horse down after the wild ride.

"Be quiet, otherwise I will get a headache from your shouting! We have visitors from the village, you say? Well, then let's go greet the two tough guys. You'll like this, Ken. Ian is a very typical Scottish highland specimen!"

Angus is about to start riding when Ken replies without emotion, "I know very well who Ian

MacDonald is... He was one of the reasons why my mother left Scotland at the time..."

Chapter 100

With slow, elegant steps, Linda walks to the door in front of which the border policeman is standing. She stops shortly before reaching him and turns around slowly. She looks into the piercing green eyes, which stare right back. Slowly her lips open and she whispers so softly that he can barely hear what she's saying and yet loudly enough that he understands her words in Swiss German.

"You will never see MY daughter again in your life. You will no longer steal babies or sell children. You will no longer be able to touch or hurt any woman... I have waited for this moment of revenge for more than 13 years and I have imagined everything down to the last detail." She pauses briefly and closes her eyes as if she feels the need to look at those horrible images again and internalize the memories. Suddenly, her eyes open, and she shakes her head as she adds, no longer in a whisper, "But all

I feel is pity for a broken creature. Simon, I forgive you for what you did to my body, my soul and mind because of your love for my husband. I thank you for my wonderful new family and indescribable friends. And soon, very soon, I will have the chance to meet my biological daughter and help her get over the terrible pain that you caused her, too. But you know, Simon," she says his name emphatically and continues, "the terrible pain you have caused has become upon which our family has grown in love and mutual respect. That has kept me alive and will help our girl flourish. Thanks to you, she has a wonderful sister and stronger, more determined parents than she would have had. You only get rich when you have something that money can't buy. Take care, Simon Zimmermann."

She turns to the door, which the police officer is now opening, and looks back over her shoulder. "Isn't it terrible to misunderstand something as wonderful as love?" She takes a deep breath and walks into the cool corridor with her head held high. She hears the door closing behind her, a key turning in the lock, the sounds of a chair being thrown against a wall with full force, and the loud sobbing of a broken man.

"I am now ready to see the girl..."

Linda walks over to the next door with the border policeman. She closes her eyes briefly and then nods to her companion with determination. He opens the door and Linda walks through. She looks into the big, green and fearful eyes of a pale teenage girl. Her heart beats faster and she feels a wave of happiness rise up inside her.

"Hello Mirjam. Nice to finally get to meet you. My name is Linda Jasmin Steiner. May I sit next to you?"

Chapter 101

"Rosalía!!!" Ken's loud shouting echoes all over the entire property. He rides his horse into the yard, jumps quickly from the saddle and runs to the center of the gravel area. A tall, heavy man lies on his stomach on the ground, swearing, and on his back sits the small, very fit Mexican woman, holding his hands crossed over each other.

"Hola mi amor! Look who I have here! May I introduce; Ian MacDonald! Without burgers and fries!" She laughs confidently and grins triumphantly at her husband.

"Have you gone crazy!? What are you doing?! And where are...?!" Disturbed and irritated, Kenneth looks around and sees a policeman standing with his arms crossed next to the veterinarian, who is also standing still.

"Sir Conley, I assume?" The policeman approaches the lawyer with an outstretched hand. "It's just Mr. Conley... What's going on here, Officer?! What is my wife doing sitting on Mr. MacDonald and why are you just watching?" He also looks at Stacy, who seems distracted by someone else. Ken looks in her direction and sees Angus, who is pressing his lips tightly together. Suddenly his lips part and a loud, hearty laugh bursts from the flushed face of the handsome Scotsman. He slaps his thigh with full force and walks with loud steps over the gravel path towards the other two men.

"Is there more of her kind where she comes from?! Your little Mexican woman has really got something, nephew, something like what people here in this country used to have." He grabs Ken's shoulder and looks down at the policeman. "James? To what do we owe this honor?" He keeps looking at Rosalía and the angry Ian lying under her.

"Damn it, MacKay! Tell this crazy woman to get off me! She's insane! She's rabid! Come on! James! I will report this in Glasgow! Now get off, you... You...!!!"

At these words, Rosalia pulls his arms briefly but violently up from his back, which makes him cry out in pain. Then she bends over and whispers in his ear, "Miss Conley to you, you Scottish disgrace! Too bad for you that you get the brunt of all my rage from the past few weeks! And now cálmete!!! My children are taking a nap and woe to you if you wake them up!"

The policeman says, "Ian MacDonald actually wanted to snitch on you about the fact that you left the property to go to the airport... Then on the way here, the stupid man opened his big mouth and exposed the lies he told as a witness regarding Dunn. And when we asked about you here, this adorable lady became self-employed in a flash." He points with his hand at Rosalía, who is beaming with joy. "I assume that Sam already discovered us on the way here, since you two got here so fast. Angus Cunningham MacKay, I hereby officially withdraw the charges against you. The case of the Duncan Dunn's cause of death is hereby closed and will be dismissed as a tragic accident due to excessive alcohol consumption."

Chapter 102

"Stop it!! I am neither old nor handicapped nor lazy! You should teach yourself manners, buddy!" Susan Manders grabs her purse from the airport attendant and can barely restrain herself from punching him. Horrified, she takes a final look at the wheelchair provided for her and walks through the private arrivals area with her head raised theatrically. She pulls her cell phone out of her purse and presses a speed dial button. "You will not believe what they had here for me when I got off the plane. If that was your decision, then I swear to our Lord in heaven, the things I'm going to do to your handsome face, Mister Universe!" She snorts these words angrily, and then smiles into the small phone at her ear. She nods, apparently soothed as she listens to the person she is talking to. Then she answers his question, saying, "I thought so... Yes, I'll be right out. What are you wearing so that I can recognize you?" Laughing, she clicks the conversation away and walks through the door that opens magically before her.

"Come here, my spy! Let me give you a hug!" With his arms spread wide, the once world-famous action hero stands a few steps away from her. As Conley warmly closes his friend in his arms and squeezes her tightly, she begins to purr softly like a cat. Amused and happy, Conley immediately squeezes her more tightly in his arms and is interrupted by a coughing fit.

253

"OK, OK..." Susie pulls away from him and coughs into her hand. "I already know that you missed me, but you don't need to break this sexy woman! My God, you still have quite a bit of strength in your old age!" She gently hits him on the arm with her purse and coughs one last time into her open hand.

"And now tell me what's going on down there! I can't reach a soul at that border bunker and the gunman wearing a suit didn't want to give me any information. Imagine – they put me in the police car like a felon!" She keeps shaking her head as they slowly walk towards the gate.

"Well, you weren't completely innocent yourself, my demonstrator!" Frank gives her a loving push on the side and winks at her.

"Pfff... The joint had to be mixed up somehow down there! Hey, I tell you! You should have seen the nasty guy, trembling with fear! And the psychiatrist first, was his face ever red..." As she continues babbling excitedly, she suddenly realizes that she has no idea where she is going. She looks around and looks at her faithful companion. "New gate? Am I getting on another plane somewhere? Are you now banishing me to the remote island with the many super fit male models?" Manders purses her lips in curiosity and raises one eyebrow.

Frank throws his head back and laughs out loud. "Susan Manders! You should become a screenwriter; your imagination is ready to make movies!" He claps his hands, an adventurous look in his eyes, and stops.

"Even worse! I am now taking you to the promised land, where the men run around in skirts and no underpants and where savages ride their horses!"

Chapter 103

Happy with herself and the world, Rosalía gazes at the crackling fire in the fireplace. She sips from her pewter mug filled with whisky and closes her eyes when she feels the golden liquid on her tongue.

"Well, I have to admit that I've never seen anything like it. A woman who throws men twice her size onto the ground and then drinks whisky from a tin mug. Is everyone like that in Mexico?" Angus shakes his head barely noticeably and hands Stacy a whisky glass. Rosalía smiles and does not take her eyes off the fire.

"I am an exception in many areas. Before I got to know Ken and gave birth to the two burritos, I was a super sporty, self-talking loner who plunged into Scottish medieval novels night after night. So this country became a fantasy haven for me. I swore to myself, should I ever get here, I would drink my whisky from a tin cup. Unfortunately, it never worked out for me to get a job here. But what heaven has given me, Díos mío, I never even dared to dream of!" She giggles happily into her tin mug and takes a hearty sip from it.

"Everything seems to be working out for all of us! It's almost a cliché, isn't it?" Stacy looks at her Angus with love, and raising her glass, adds, "Now let's hope for good news from your friends in Mexico!" All three take a sip of their drinks and stare into the blazing flames.

256

Hailey and Bonnie come into the cozy living room holding one full tray each and set the large table. "You can't just drink, you need to get some nutritious food into your stomachs also!" Hailey gives Angus a reproachful look. "You have to take care of our guests, Angus Cunningham MacKay! Not everyone is made of leather butts and whisky stomachs!" Bonnie giggles at these words and whispers, "Our Rose always said that to father..."

"Well, I definitely don't have a leather butt! Mine is already freezing!" Amused, Kenneth Conley steps into the living room and shows off his traditional Scottish outfit. He makes a knightly bow and winks at his surprised wife. She whoops and claps her hands enthusiastically. "Mi héroe escocés!!!"

Suddenly a large mural falls to the floor and the earth seems to vibrate. Everyone looks around and at each other in confusion.

Outro

"Mrs. Steiner? Mrs. Steiner?" Jasmin opens her eyes in alarm. "I'm sorry to have to wake you up, but we're already in our descent for the landing. May I ask you to put your backrest upright?" The neatly dressed flight attendant gives her business passenger an enchanting smile.

"Oh, yes, of course!" Jasmin blinks sleepily and leans her head back on the seat. It slowly moves back to a vertical sitting position and she looks around, irritated. She quickly pushes the blanket off her lap and grabs her rounded stomach with both hands. She closes her eyes again briefly, takes a deep breath and exhales it audibly.

"You had an admirably deep sleep! And you had some wild dreams, too!" A mature lady seated across the aisle gives her a happy wink. Jasmin gives her a questioning look." You... You are from Scotland?!"

"Oh, yes, my dear, I told you that before you fell into dreamland. When you started watching that horrible baby kidnapping movie with Sir Conley. He's

258

from the same place in the Scottish Highlands as I am. Don't you remember anymore?" She tries to hold her hand in Jasmin's direction, but realizes that the distance is too great.

"Is everything all right, my dear? You look so distraught. Were you having a nightmare?" The woman blinks sympathetically at her pregnant flight neighbor and adds, with concern, "Do you still know who you are and where you want to go, dear?"

"Yes, luckily I remember that... My name is Jasmin Steiner, I'm Swiss and I'm on my way to New York to meet up with my husband who is visiting an old friend..." As she finishes speaking, she caresses her belly gently.

"And together you will travel to Mexico to spend a few vacation days in a beautiful tree house hotel! You also told me that. Oh, I'm glad, my dear, that everything is fine with you! You just scared me a bit. That most definitely must be the hormones."

Jasmin smiles in relief at the well-groomed lady and nods in agreement. "Me, too..." Again, she strokes her rounded stomach gently and says,

"Unfortunately, my dream made me very confused. What was your name again??"

"It's OK, dear! The same thing happens to me without any dreams or pregnancy hormones! I gave you my card, you put it in on your cell phone case." The nice woman with a Scottish accent winks at Jasmin with amusement and points next to Jasmin her finger. She reaches for the card, which is peeking out of her cell phone case and looks at it. She grins with a shake of her head and reads aloud, "Susan Manders, bestselling author and health coach."

"I would love to hear from you as soon as your baby is born! It will definitely be a gorgeous boy! Do you already have a name for him??"

Jasmin looks out of her window at the New York City skyline.

"Kenneth or Angus sound good to me…"

***

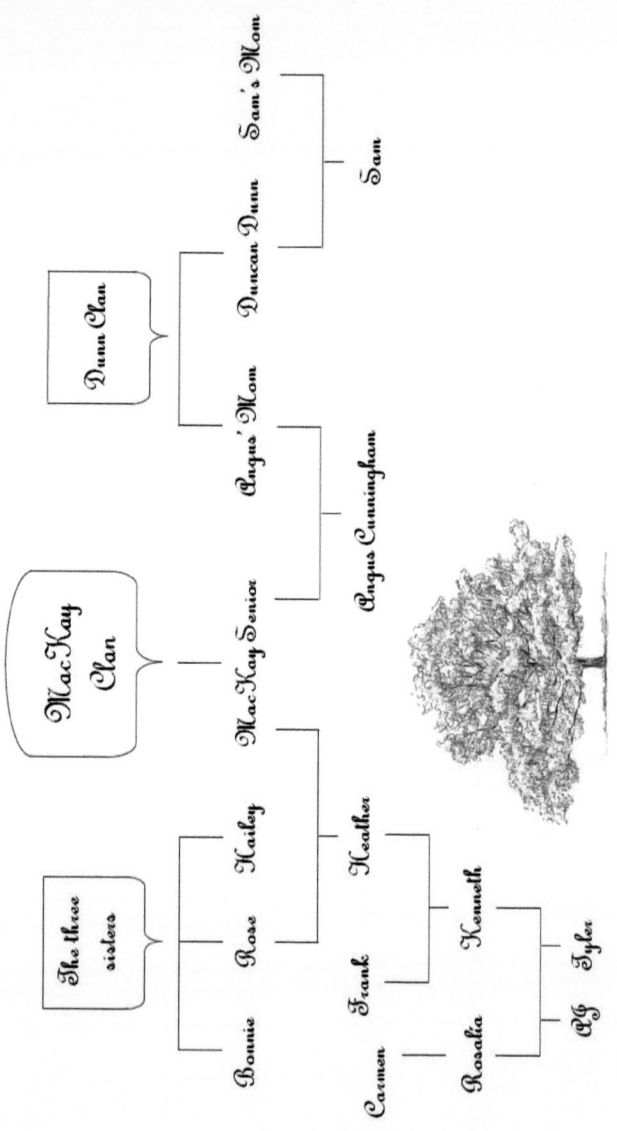

The three sisters

Bonnie   Rose   Hailey

MacKay Clan

MacKay Senior

Angus' Mom

Duncan Dunn

Sam's Mom

Dunn Clan

Carmen   Frank   Heather   Kenneth

Angus Cunningham

Sam

Rosalia   PJ   Tyler

"I would like to thank Nicholas and Romano and, of course, all my readers for their loyal support of this story. With a tear in my eye, I have to say goodbye to these characters, who have been with me for years now! With a twinkle in my eye, I am looking forward to writing another, hopefully equally exciting story for all of you."

Hasta luego and Slàinte Mhaht!

Hiam Mondini